Carol said, "I'll see you to the front door and then look around outside to make sure everything's all right."

Sybil was suddenly aware that she must have a gun with her, and the sense of danger, absent all day, rushed back to surround her.

The stone steps were slippery from the warm rain and it was so dark that Sybil had difficulty seeing her way. "Be careful," she said over her shoulder. She was acutely aware of Carol directly behind her on the steps, so when she slipped it was not surprising to find Carol's arm supporting her. What astonished Sybil was her own reaction. She found herself turning within the half embrace, until their lips met so naturally that Sybil had melted into the kiss before she realized exactly what was happening. Then it was too late to stop, too late to think, too late to be sensible. In the darkness they kissed urgently, passionately, Carol's arms tight around her.

Alarm began to ring insistently in Sybil's mind. Burning, she thrust Carol away, broke the circle of her arms, and fled up the wet steps to the front door. Carol didn't follow. Sybil fumbled with the key and finally wrenched the door open. She turned on the outside light to dispel the dangerous darkness. Jeffrey darted up the steps, wound around Sybil's legs and then walked delicately inside. From below Carol's clear voice said, "Sybil? Are you all right?"

ABOUT THE AUTHOR

CLAIRE MCNAB is the author of fifteen Detective Inspector Carol Ashton mysteries: *Lessons in Murder, Fatal Reunion, Death Down Under, Cop Out, Dead Certain, Body Guard, Double Bluff, Inner Circle, Chain Letter, Past Due, Set Up, Under Suspicion, Death Club, Accidental Murder* and *Blood Link*. She has written two romances, *Under the Southern Cross* and *Silent Heart*, and has co-authored a self-help book, *The Loving Lesbian*, with Sharon Gedan. She is the author of four Denise Cleever thrillers, *Murder Undercover, Death Understood, Out of Sight*, and *Recognition Factor*.

An Australian now living permanently in Los Angeles, she teaches fiction writing in the UCLA Extension Writers' Program. She makes it a point to return once a year to Australia to refresh her Aussie accent.

Lessons In
Murder

The first Detective Inspector Carol Ashton Mystery

CLAIRE
McNAB

Bella
BOOKS
2004

Bella Books, Inc.
P.O. Box 10543
Tallahassee, FL 32302

First published 1988 by Naiad Press

Printed in the United States of America on acid-free paper

Editor: Katherine V. Forrest and Becky Ellis
Cover designer: Sandy Knowles

ISBN 1-931513-65-1

Chapter One

Cassie Turnbull leaned forward, sweaty hands on her grubby knees. She stared at the half-open eye and slack jaw. "He's dead," she breathed.

There was a fleeting hush in the crowd of students jostling to get a view from the doorway of the woodwork room. "You sure?" said one. Cassie edged closer and extended an exploratory finger.

She rose, freckles standing out on her white face. "Yeah. We'd better get Farrell."

The body had ceased to be Mr. Pagett, Industrial Arts teacher: now it was the central piece of a drama. Although momentarily awed by the sight of their teacher's sprawled form, some students were already visualizing the satisfyingly startled faces of friends and families; others entertained the pleasant thought that normal lessons would probably be suspended for the rest of the day.

* * * * *

Mrs. Farrell watched her teaching staff enter the common room with very little of her usual pleasure. February was a trying month at the best of times, with reluctant students returning after the long break to swelter in classrooms while the Sydney summer delivered perfect day after perfect day of burnished heat. Now, barely two weeks into the first term of the year, this event threatened to not only disrupt the smooth running of her school, but to bring most unwelcome publicity. The identity of the dead teacher had galvanized both the Education Department and the police into impressive action.

She glanced curiously at the woman who sat beside her. Inspector Carol Ashton's spectacular career had not been hindered by her cool blonde good looks. Mrs. Farrell looked at the tanned skin, sleek hair, firm mouth, and direct green eyes so familiar from television newscasts, and smiled grimly to herself. Carol Ashton would not be put on any ordinary, grubby murder case. Her presence was a testament to the power of political influence. Mrs. Farrell wondered when the dead man's illustrious father would make his appearance. She had no doubt it would be soon.

2

As Mrs. Farrell rose, an attentive silence fell upon the common room. "For any person who may not be aware of what has necessitated this sudden meeting, I regret to say that Mr. William Pagett has been found dead in his classroom in unusual circumstances."

Sybil Quade sat numbly, ignoring the murmur that greeted Mrs. Farrell's words. She already knew more than most of her colleagues. Sybil had the curious feeling that she had been an invalid for a long time, although only a few hours ago she had been striding confidently to the administration block through the hot February morning. Mrs. Farrell had emerged from Bill's woodwork room, jaw clamped tight with shock, and had called her over to supervise and isolate the class from the rest of the school while the police were called. Sybil had sat mutely in the principal's office, letting the excited students sit on the thick green carpet and talk to each other. It would have been impossible to keep them quiet.

Sybil was consumed with a frightening desire to know every detail. The fragments of description, the hushed voices, the muffled exclamations of horrified delight — all these had built up in her imagination a vivid picture. Last night that body had moved with energy and violence. Now it lay, silent and undignified, the blood settling slowly in its limbs and the processes of decay inevitably beginning. Sybil watched without interest as a blonde woman rose to address the meeting. She looked like a successful executive — cool, decisive, disciplined, and in complete control.

Sybil's thoughts resumed their frantic kaleidoscope. Her fingers traced the welt along her cheekbone. Had it been only last night? She felt an odd detachment, as though watching a replay on a screen: she heard the vicious words, the splintering glass, the squeal of tires as

3

she roared down Bill's precipitous driveway and skidded onto the road.

The picture was broken by the sound of the blonde woman speaking. She had an arresting voice — clear, silvery, and effortlessly pitched to reach every person in the crowded room.

Sybil felt the steady pressure of Terry's arm against her body. She moved slightly, but he shifted to maintain contact with her bare arm. "Watch this one," he said quietly. "Very high-powered, very successful, very confident. A mean bitch." Alarm began to ring in Sybil's mind. She forced herself to listen closely as the woman continued.

"I'm sure you'll understand there are certain procedures to be followed in these circumstances that may cause some inconvenience. As a matter of routine we will be taking fingerprints, for example, and also asking you to accept a temporary restriction of your movements. In particular, if you wish to leave the school premises will you please advise the police officer in the main office of this administration block. We hope to complete most of the preliminary interviews today. In addition we will be requiring access to certain areas, and will be approaching you individually on this."

"You know what that means?" said Terry loudly enough for everyone to hear. "Search warrants. Cops pawing through personal belongings."

The Inspector gave him a level glance, then turned away to speak to Mrs. Farrell. The meeting broke up in a hubbub of exclamations, teachers spilling out into the brassy midday sun in twos or threes. Sybil drifted outside without conscious volition. She felt like a jellyfish floating slackly in a warm sea.

4

"Walk!" A hand under her elbow and steady pressure to move forward. Sybil turned her head and her eyes met Terry's. His black glance was, as always, opaque. "You'll get sunstroke if you stand out here much longer. Come on."

As they drew near the English staff room he slowed, tightening his fingers on her arm. "About last night, Syb," he said urgently, "don't say anything about seeing Bill. No one knows about it. You'd only cause yourself trouble if you mention it. The police won't understand." His eyes shifted to her cheek. "He hit you, did he?"

Sybil stared at him, but before she could answer a young and self-important voice broke in, a junior student bursting with the importance of his task, so far removed from the usual boring school messages. "Mrs. Quade? It's urgent."

Sybil looked at the note on the clipboard. She was summoned to the principal's office for an interview.

Chapter Two

"Mrs. Quade?" said Carol Ashton, rising from the principal's chair. "Please sit down." She was struck by Sybil Quade's attractiveness.

Sybil waited, acutely aware of everything in the room. A trapped blowfly buzzed against the window, the curtains moved lazily in the breeze, the Inspector's calm green eyes regarded her objectively.

"Detective Bourke will be making notes of our conversation."

The man sitting attentively to one side of the desk had an unremarkably pleasant face. He gave Sybil a faint smile. She did not return it.

Carol Ashton's clear voice caught her attention. "This is your current staff information sheet. Are the details still correct?"

"Yes."

"You're separated from your husband, Mrs. Quade?" She watched Sybil Quade with heightening interest.

"I don't see . . ." Sybil paused, then continued, "yes. Tony went back to England at the end of last year."

"Your husband is British?"

"Yes." Silence stretched, to be filled. Sybil cleared her throat. "I haven't spoken to Tony for . . ." She trailed off, remembering their last heated argument.

Carol Ashton consulted papers. Bourke wrote in his notebook. Sybil felt the heavy beat of her heart. The cool green eyes met hers.

"How well did you know Bill Pagett?"

"Quite well. He was my husband's friend in the first place. I met him for the first time at Bill's house. Look, I really don't know what this has to do with everything."

Carol said deliberately, "When did you last see Mr. Pagett — alive?"

That was meant to shock, and it did. "I'm not sure. This morning, I think, but I don't remember speaking to him."

"Would you regard Mr. Pagett as a close, personal friend?"

"Bill? Not a close friend, no."

"So he was your husband's friend, not yours?"

"I suppose so." Sybil looked up to Carol Ashton's raised eyebrows. "Yes," she added flatly, "Bill was Tony's

friend. Bill and I teach at the same school, but we don't
... we didn't ... have much in common."

"Except your husband."

"Except Tony."

Another long pause. Sybil looked at the sleek blonde
hair and clean planes of Carol Ashton's face. She heard
Terry's words: a mean bitch. She waited, suspended, for
the next question.

Carol watched her. "Did Mr. Pagett appear quite
normal when you last saw him? Was he agitated or angry,
perhaps?"

Sybil thought of his contorted face as he had shouted
at her last night. "No, I didn't notice anything." Was the
Inspector satisfied, convinced? Sybil couldn't tell from her
expression.

"We have been informed that Mr. Pagett was
responsible for your separation from your husband," she
said.

The blowfly still buzzed maddeningly at the window.
"Who told you that?"

Another interminable pause. Sybil knew that the
silence was designed to make her talk. Even so, she
couldn't bear to let it stretch any longer. "Tony and I
agreed to separate because we found we were no longer
happy together. Bill had nothing to do with it — he was
just Tony's friend. Tony went to stay with him after we
parted. That's all. Bill ... Bill was Tony's closest friend."

Who would leave you? thought Carol, looking at the
curve of Sybil's mouth and the line of her cheekbones.
Aloud, she said, "Did you speak to Bill Pagett last night?"

"No, I didn't see him."

"Did you telephone Bill Pagett?"

"No." Sybil licked dry lips. "Look, can I ask you
something?"

8

"Of course."

"It is murder, isn't it? Not just some dreadful accident?"

"Not an accident. No." Carol Ashton watched her steadily across the desk, waiting. Detective Bourke looked up from his notebook. Neither showed any surprise at her next question.

"What happened?" Sybil searched for words. "It's not just curiosity. I sat in his office for more than an hour this morning, looking after the kids who found him. I didn't even try to stop them whispering to each other. What I mean is, whatever I can imagine must be worse than what actually happened. I'm sure of that."

Afterwards Sybil wondered why the information was given to her so freely, but now she listened tensely as the silvery voice said, "It's only a preliminary report, but it appears likely that Mr. Pagett was first knocked unconscious by a blow to his head. . . ." She paused. "Sure you want to hear this? It's not very pleasant."

Sybil felt an insane desire to laugh. "Is it ever pleasant?" she said. "I'm sorry. I just . . . please go on."

The calm voice continued inexorably. "It looks very much as if someone took a power drill and used it to go up through the base of his skull and into his brain."

"They drilled a hole in his head?" Sybil stood up. "I'm sorry — I can't stay. Excuse me."

The blowfly buzzed against the window in the silence Sybil left behind her. Carol stood up and scooped it to freedom through the bottom of the window. "What do you thing?" she asked Bourke.

"I think we should ask her how she got that rather spectacular bruise," said Bourke with a grin. "Redheads like her have fiery tempers — who knows what she might do if pushed too far?"

9

"Who knows, indeed," said Carol Ashton, sardonically amused that both she and Bourke felt the same pull of physical attraction towards Sybil Quade. No. Forget it, she told herself.

* * * * *

Lunchtime at Bellwhether High was green and grey uniforms, ball games, sandwiches, chatter, clumps of kids, overflowing rubbish bins, the sound of surf in the distance. Summer had scorched the grass and faded the cloudless sky pale blue. The eucalyptus gums hung their grey-green leaves in the breathless heat but the air was alive with a buzz of gossip, innuendo and speculation as, by some strange osmosis, every student of Bellwhether High seemed to know exactly what had happened.

Mrs. Farrell was in the main office announcing strategies to the office staff for dealing with the media assault that had already lit up every line on the switchboard when Sir Richard Pagett strode into the room. His famous face was strained, but his equally famous charm was intact. "Mrs. Farrell. Phyllis, isn't it? We met when William first came to the school."

Mrs. Farrell murmured appropriate words of condolence as she ushered Sir Richard to the deputy principal's office. "The police are using my room for interviews," she explained.

"Is Carol Ashton here?"

"Yes. Do you wish to see her?"

"Not at the moment."

Sir Richard was slightly below average height, but he radiated such confidence and power that he seemed much taller. His head of thick white hair, crisp voice and electric smile were instantly recognizable to every citizen in the state, as befitted the product of a massive public relations system. Rumors of corruption had dogged his final years as one of the state's longest serving Premiers, but he had finally retired with honors and fulsome praise two years previously. He was still constantly in the public eye, not only because of his string of racehorses and his spectacular betting plunges but, less fortunately, because of allegations made to several royal commissions about his involvement in organized crime.

All this was in Mrs. Farrell's thoughts as Sir Richard leaned forward in the chair to say, "Phyllis, I know you realize what a dreadful shock this has been. William was my youngest son. For this to happen is almost beyond belief. That is why I'm sure you understand if I ask you to do something for me."

Although instantly wary, Mrs. Farrell maintained an expression of sympathetic interest as he continued, "I know you will fully cooperate with Inspector Ashton, that goes without saying, but I want to ask you to do a little more." He took a card from his wallet and placed it firmly in her hand. "Here is my personal telephone number. Of course, it's unlisted, and I would ask that you keep it confidential. I want you to call me, day or night, if you learn anything at all about my son. Normally I'd never listen to common gossip, but in this situation any detail, any information at all, is of importance to me."

"Surely if I tell Inspector Ashton. . . ."

"Of course. But quite apart from the information you will be giving her, there may be little details, speculation, suspicions or thoughts that you might have — things that are too flimsy to be called facts — anything that could conceivably relate to my son — I'd like to hear it."

Leaving, he paused at the doorway of the office. "And, Phyllis — I know I can rely on your complete discretion."

11

* * * * *

When Sybil opened the door of the English staff room she was immediately the focus of attention. The familiar faces seemed disconcertingly strange, as if she were seeing them for the first time. Terry stared at her with his usual black, intense gaze, his powerful, compact form giving an impression of energy barely under control. Lynne was smoothing her cap of glossy dark hair; her deep pink dress was immaculate, her makeup perfect, her expression an appropriate one of brave grief. Edwina's large body filled her chair, her pretty face losing definition at her jawline and flowing into the generous curves of her body. In contrast, Alan Witcombe, head of the English Department, sat prim and angular, his mouth tight as he ran a hand over his thinning hair. The only person who moved was Pete. His soft, open face concerned, he led Sybil to the central table, sat her down with a cup of coffee, and then leaned against a filing cabinet, nervously smoothing his new mustache.

"Syb, you look absolutely dreadful," said Lynne, flashing her gold bangles in an expansive gesture. "And what have you done to your face?"

"Just a stupid accident — I hit myself with the edge of a cupboard door in the kitchen."

"Oh?" said Lynne, obviously unconvinced. "Looks like someone slapped you."

"You've been watching too many soap operas," said Terry sourly.

Lynne ignored him. "I gather, Syb, Inspector Carol Ashton lives up to her tough reputation. You look positively green."

"What happened?" said Terry, seizing the opportunity to put his arm around Sybil's shoulders.

12

She shrugged him off. "Nothing much," she said, "I just threw up when she told me about Bill, about how...."

"Not in the principal's office! Not on Farrell's green pile carpet?" asked Edwina in surprised delight, hoisting herself from her chair.

Sybil shook her head. "No, I made it to the washroom." She sank down at her desk, wishing everyone would go away.

"What made you vomit?" asked Lynne with lively interest.

"Leave her alone!" snapped Terry.

"Sybil doesn't have the monopoly on shock," said Lynne, irritated, "I feel Bill's death deeply. After all, Bill and I were *friends,* which is more than Sybil can say."

Terry was furious. "What's that supposed to mean?" he asked, striding across to Lynne who was checking her reflection in a mirror placed rakishly on an overflowing bookcase.

Lynne swung around with equal anger. "Look, Terry, don't try and push me around. Everyone knows there was no love lost between Sybil and Bill. It's natural the police would be interested. That's their job, poking and prying into other people's business."

"You just do it for a hobby, Lynne, do you?" asked Edwina.

"Honestly, Edwina, you can be a perfect bitch," Lynne drawled, shaking a bottle of purple-red nail polish with languid vigor. "Frankly, I can't wait to have my interview with the famous Inspector Carol Ashton. With a bit of luck, we'll all be on television. After all, not only do we have the Inspector the media love to love, we also have Bill's father. *He's* famous enough in his own right."

13

The bell rang to signal the start of afternoon lessons. When no one moved, Alan, always conscious of his position as head of the English Department, roused them with admonitions. "Come on, everyone. You know what the kids will be like after what's happened. Control, we must keep control. Please go to class promptly."

"I have a free period," said Sybil.

The others left with various shades of reluctance, except for Terry. He stood behind Sybil's chair, his hands resting on her shoulders. He said, "Why did you go to see Bill last night?"

"How do you know I saw Bill?"

Terry's hands tightened. "It doesn't matter how I know. What did you tell that woman?"

Sybil sighed with weariness. "I took your advice. I said I didn't see Bill last night."

"Tell me about it so I can help you. That Inspector won't let it rest, you know. She'll keep asking questions. She'll ferret away until she gets something. She likes success. She won't care about you."

"Leave me alone!" said Sybil with a savagery that surprised them both.

"Tony isn't back, is he?"

Sybil swung around, astonished. "Tony? You know he's in England. What makes you think he's here?"

The phone rang. Exclaiming impatiently, Terry snatched it up. "What? Oh, all right. As soon as I can. Look, I said I'd come, okay?" He slammed the receiver down. "The Gestapo want me for my interview," he said to Sybil. He took her hands. "Don't worry, Syb. I won't say anything about last night."

You always want me to owe you something, thought Sybil as she watched him leave.

14

*****

Bellwhether High was a showpiece school, often used by the Education Department to impress overseas educational experts and sundry dignitaries. It was set in a large expanse of landscaped grounds close to the spectacular sandstone cliffs and beaches of the Peninsula area north of Sydney. At times this was a disadvantage, because when the surf was up, the attendance was often down. The school itself was made up of a series of courtyards, each bounded by two stories of classrooms. Concrete causeways connected the upper stories of each separate block, covered walkways the lower. At the northern end of the site was the administration block, bearing on its face huge letters proclaiming Bellwhether High School, strategically placed so that it could be easily read by those travelling on the major coast highway.

Cynics said the unaccustomed luxury of this government school was related to the fact that it was located in a marginal seat and electors had to be bought or bribed. True or not, a state government election had coincided with Bellwhether's official opening by Sir Richard Pagett shortly before he retired. Much mileage had been given to the fact that Sir Richard's youngest son, Bill, was joining the Industrial Arts staff — proof positive that the state government supported public education. The electorate dutifully returned the appropriate member of Sir Richard's party and Bellwhether High faded from the news until the Monday when Bill Pagett died.

Mrs. Farrell stood uneasily in Workroom 2 with Carol Ashton and Jim Madigan, the head of the Industrial Arts Department. The body had been removed, but the chalk outline was an uncomfortable reminder of the near panic

15

she had felt when she found Bill Pagett slumped on the floor.

"Really, Inspector, do you need me here?" she asked.

"It would be a help."

There was no answer to that. Mrs. Farrell waited grimly as Carol Ashton questioned Jim Madigan. "Are these sliding doors to the room kept locked when there's no class in here?"

Madigan shot a look at Mrs. Farrell. "Well. . . ."

"They certainly should be," said Mrs. Farrell tartly. "Those are my instructions, but I'm afraid they are not always followed, even though tools and the like are easily stolen."

The Inspector indicated the preparation room that served as a connection between Workrooms 1 and 2. "In a similar way I imagine the preparation room doors are supposed to be kept locked?"

"In a similar way no doubt they are not," said Mrs. Farrell with irritation. Madigan looked glum.

"So someone could enter this workroom at any time, either through these sliding glass doors that the students use, or through the preparation room from Workroom 1?"

"Obviously, yes," said Mrs. Farrell, thinking of the last Industrial Arts inventory. Madigan had the grace to look embarrassed, but she was sure he took the continual loss of valuable equipment far less seriously than she did.

Madigan cleared his throat. "I've heard a Black and Decker drill . . ." he began, trailing off into a red-faced silence.

Mrs. Farrell glared at him. The man was a fool, but she had never had much time for his department anyway and, as for Bill Pagett, she had paid him very little attention until the anonymous letters had started arriving. Even then, Bill Pagett had never known about

16

them, so her acquaintance with him had been essentially superficial. She had already decided to ignore the subject of the letters. No one else knew about them, and she had enough problems without adding to the list. Besides, she had destroyed the nasty things.

Her thoughts were broken by Carol Ashton's clear voice. "Mrs. Farrell?"

"Sorry. Yes?"

"Both you and Mr. Madigan saw the drill by the body's head. Could any of the students have touched it?"

Mrs. Farrell permitted herself a wintry smile. "I imagine you've met Cassie Turnbull, who discovered the body. She's well known to me, unfortunately, because of her aversion to discipline of any kind. However, having been brought up on a steady diet of television crime, I doubt very much if she would allow anyone to touch anything. In fact, she surprised me by the way she took charge of the class when she realized what had happened. It showed leadership I had, frankly, not suspected before."

Mrs. Farrell winced when Carol Ashton showed a Polaroid photograph of Bill Pagett's head with his half-open dead eye staring at the point of the drill. She agreed with Madigan that the position of the drill corresponded with her memory.

"You can see it was pointed at his eye," said Madigan, looking sick. "Are you telling us someone drilled into his head, then arranged it that way?"

"Yes," said Carol Ashton.

* * * * *

Even before Carol Ashton had reached the top of the drive she could hear angry voices. She turned and looked

17

back towards the sea, listening closely. The air was still, hot and clear, and the white breakers rolled with delightful precision to the shore. The heated words were indistinct, so after a moment she went up the stone steps and rang the bell. The voices stopped.

"Mrs. Quade. Sorry to interrupt you at home, but our interview was cut short, and I'd like to get your statement completed so it can be typed and signed." Carol was inside with practiced ease, nodding pleasantly to Terry, who stood behind Sybil.

Terry's face was too carefully blank. "I'll stay," he said to Sybil. She shook her head. He hesitated. "I'll ring you later, okay?" Ignoring Carol, he lingered reluctantly on the steps, then slowly walked down the drive, looking back.

Carol refused a drink, accepted a seat, opened a notebook. The room was flooded with light and air, the house set so high that the wide glass doors opened to a stunning view of headlands, sea and sky. "You said your husband was still in England?" she said mildly, her eyes on the line of the horizon where the two blues met.

"Tony? I think so, yes. We don't keep in contact."

"You haven't heard from him?"

"No. Why?"

Carol knew the value of silence. She smiled pleasantly, and watched Sybil closely. You're a knockout, she thought, enjoying the long line of thigh revealed by the white canvas pants. A large ginger cat stalked into the room, inspected Carol imperiously, and amused her by swishing his tail dismissively and stalking out again.

Sybil ran her fingers through her short curly red hair. "Why are you asking me about Tony? What has it got to do with . . . what's happened?"

Carol consulted her notebook. "Passport control shows that your husband entered Australia through Melbourne airport a week ago." A pause, then, mildly: "You haven't spoken to him?"

Sybil looked away, biting her lip. "No."

"Would you have expected him to contact you?"

Sybil looked up to meet Carol's steady green gaze. "I don't know."

"Is there any reason why he would go to Melbourne, and not Sydney? It's over a thousand kilometers away."

"Tony has friends there. When he first came to Australia he lived in Melbourne. He said the climate was more like the one he was used to, but after he'd visited Sydney a couple of times, he moved north."

"You haven't heard from any of his friends in Melbourne?"

"No. I've told you I haven't."

Carol's expression didn't change at the note of anger in Sybil's voice. What are you hiding? she thought. She let the silence last a moment, then said, "You've hurt your face."

"Yes, I banged it on a cupboard door."

"This morning?"

"Yes," said Sybil firmly. She glanced at the open notebook. "Why are you interested, anyway?"

Carol didn't answer her question, flicking over a few pages, and saying, "As I mentioned in our first interview, we've been told your relationship with Bill Pagett was the reason you and your husband separated."

"That's not true."

Carol raised her eyebrows. "The person was very positive." Don't lie to me, she thought.

Sybil flushed with anger. "Does everyone tell you the truth?"

"Of course not. Some people lie outright, or twist things to put themselves in a favorable light, or to try to get even with someone they dislike. I'm not taking this information on face value. I'm asking you if it's true."

"It's not." Did Carol Ashton believe her? Did she think she was lying? Sybil stood up, determined to end the interview; but Carol remained sitting, steadily surveying her. Terry had left his cigarettes, and although she rarely smoked, Sybil fumbled, lit one, and coughed as she inhaled.

"Have you instituted divorce proceedings? No? How long ago did you separate?"

"What has this got to do with Bill? What does it matter whether I divorce my husband or not?"

Carol looked sympathetic. "I'm sorry to have to ask these questions. I know they intrude into your personal life, but in a case like this, I'm afraid they're essential."

Sybil didn't trust her sympathy, but she was willing to play along just to get through the interview, so she replied in a calm and reasonable tone, "Tony and I separated a few months before he went back to England. The reason was quite simple — we found our marriage was a mistake — we'd grown apart. No one came between us — we just realized we were incompatible."

"All very civilized?" said Carol.

Sybil looked up sharply. Was that sarcasm? But Carol Ashton's attractive face was reflecting neutral interest.

"Very civilized," Sybil agreed.

Carol Ashton stood up. Apparently the interview was over. At the door she turned to Sybil, handing her a card. "Please keep this. When your husband contacts you, I would very much appreciate it if you would ring me immediately."

20

Sybil absently noted that Carol Ashton had beautiful hands. She took the card without comment, and watched her walk unhurriedly down the steps. At the bottom she turned. "Oh, and Mrs. Quade," she said, "just as a matter of routine, we will be requesting your permission to search your property."

Sybil stood at the open door until she was out of sight.

Chapter Three

Because Carol had woken at daybreak and gone for a run in the welcome quietness of early light, she arrived at the school before seven. Even so, the cleaners were there before her. "What time do you start?" she asked a middle-aged man in overalls.

"Five-thirty."

Carol unlocked the door to the principal's office. "Could I speak with you for a minute?"

He put down his bucket and mop and followed her into the office. She picked up the folder with the outline of the cleaning roster, smiling as she said, "I'm Inspector Carol Ashton."

"Yeah. I know."

He treated every word as if it was worth a dollar and not to be squandered, so it took her half an hour of pleasant questioning before she had all she wanted: an outline of the cleaners' responsibilities, their relationships with the staff and students and, most interesting of all, some gossip and opinions about Bill Pagett.

When Mark Bourke came in he put a folder down in front of her, saying with a grin, "There you are, boss-lady. The fruits of my midnight labors."

Carol had asked for Mark Bourke when the Commissioner had told her she could have anyone she wanted to assist her investigation. He was good-natured, painstaking, and deceptively mild when interviewing suspects: many had found to their cost how dangerous it was to underestimate him. They had worked on several cases before, and she valued the easy informality of their working relationship and the fact that Mark never made the mistake of trying to be too familiar, understanding that Carol had created a rigid division between her work and her private life.

As she opened the folder, Carol said, "Two things of interest. Had a talk with one of the cleaners this morning. Among other things, he said that a Mrs. Grunewald, who cleans Block C where the English staff room is, mentioned that she heard some kind of argument between Pagett and a senior student last Friday. She's away today sick, and it mightn't be anything important, but I think we should check it out."

"I haven't interviewed any of the cleaners yet. What's the other thing?"

23

"The medical report will arrive this morning, but I got the main points by phone, and it pretty much confirms the preliminary examination. Pagett was hit across the right side of his head with something like a length of pipe. Unfortunately nothing the scientific squad took from Pagett's woodwork room matches the dent it made. This blow almost certainly knocked him out, but it didn't kill him. The attack was probably unexpected, as there are no marks on his hands or arms, so he didn't try to protect his head. Then, some time later, possibly only a minute or so, his head was tilted forward and someone used a power drill to put a neat hole in the base of his skull. The drill penetrated its full length into his brain, killing him immediately. The Black and Decker artistically arranged by his head is the weapon — no fingerprints, but plenty of brain tissue on the drill."

"If you wanted to kill someone that way, why not drill through the side of his head?" asked Bourke, pointing to his temple. "I mean, it's much more spectacular, especially if you left the drill in place."

"Yes, I asked that. Apparently, unless you're lucky enough to hit a major blood vessel in the process, all you're likely to do is accomplish a frontal lobotomy, which might have changed Bill Pagett's personality, but wouldn't have killed him."

"You think our murderer's done some brain surgery as a hobby?" asked Bourke flippantly.

"Either by luck or intention, he or she certainly chose the most efficient point to drill a hole," said Carol, doodling interlocking circles on a notepad. "I want you to find out if anyone's got a background or special skills in anatomy or medicine or some related field."

"Okay. But why use a power drill? Look at the disadvantages: it needs a power source, it's noisy, and

24

your target has to keep still — you won't be very successful if your victim keeps dodging around."

Carol reflected, adding a series of arrows to the circles. "Perhaps a power tool symbolizes Bill Pagett, industrial arts teacher?"

"What if it's some sort of bizarre sexual thing with the Black and Decker standing in for a penis?" said Bourke with a wide grin.

"That gives new meaning to the expression, fucked in the head," said Carol drily.

"Anything else interesting?" asked Bourke, laughing.

"Yes, possibly. The body had a bruise on the left side of the jaw, as if someone had punched him, but it was a few days ago, not just before he was killed. Also there was a cut inside his mouth on the right side, but done a few hours before he died, suggesting that someone hit or slapped him," said Carol, checking the notes she had made.

"The right side would make it likely he was hit by someone left-handed. Are any of them?"

"Sybil Quade's left-handed," said Carol.

Bourke whistled. "And she looks like she traded punches with someone recently. That bruise on her left cheek is pretty bad, Carol. How did she say she got it?"

"Accident with a cupboard door."

"Believe her?"

Carol shook her head. "No," she said.

* * * * *

Alan Whitcombe's tight mouth twisted with distaste. "Have any of you read it?" he asked, waving a copy of the *Peninsula Post*. His staff looked up from their desks.

"What would you expect from a scandal sheet like this?" said Lynne, waving her copy. "Get this headline: STUDENTS SICKENED AT SLAUGHTER OF EX-PREMIER'S SON. And if that isn't enough, there's a picture of that revolting little Cassie Turnbull squinting at the camera."

"Let's have a look," said Pete. He looked considerably better as his soft, handsome face had regained its usual high color and he had stopped nervously grooming his mustache. He laughed as he read. "I don't believe it! Our Cassie has strung together a few words in a sentence or two! Hear this: Twelve-year-old Cassie Turnbull, still shocked by the gruesome discovery of her slaughtered teacher's body, told our reporter, 'It was dreadful. I felt sick all day and can never forget Mr. Pagett's dead face.' "

"Dear, dear, our Cassie's barely the sunny side of incoherent. I detect a little judicial editing there," said Edwina, dressed, as always, in a dazzlingly bright color. Today she wore orange. "She *is* in your English class, isn't she, Lynne?"

"What's that supposed to mean?"

Edwina's face showed injured innocence. "Not a thing. After all, we're only into week three of Term One, aren't we? Even a crash-hot teacher like yourself couldn't be expected to teach Cassie Turnbull the niceties of English grammar in that time." She looked at Lynne's desk. "Isn't that the cardboard I extracted from the front office? What are you doing with it?"

Lynne looked bored. "I just borrowed a few sheets."

"I need them all, Lynne. My Year Seven class is doing advertising in groups."

"How creative," said Lynne.

"Oh, stop bickering," said Terry impatiently. "Has anyone seen Sybil?"

26

"She's probably hiding somewhere, recovering from the pointed questions the police have been asking," said Lynne, languidly filing a fingernail.

"Oh?" said Edwina with raised eyebrows, "and what about you, my dear Lynne? Surely they've asked you about the way Bill dumped you for something rather younger?"

Lynne yawned. "You never do get your facts right, do you?" she said to Edwina.

* * * * *

The day had been a trying one for Mrs. Farrell. The call to her home from Sir Richard at 6:30 AM had been unwelcome, and the series of anxious parents who had insisted on speaking to her, either by telephone or in person, had been very fatiguing, especially as most of them seemed irrationally concerned that a maniac was stalking the school and their precious son or daughter could be the next victim. Even more irritating were the activities of the media. She had shuddered at the excesses of the local *Peninsula Post,* but that was nothing compared to the media assault from wide distribution newspapers, radio and television stations. The Education Department had instructed her to make no public comment, but this seemed only to intensify the efforts of the reporters who jammed the switchboard and camped outside the school entrances.

* * * * *

Bourke slid a sheet of paper in front of Carol. "We know Pagett died somewhere between eight-forty and about nine-ten, when the kids found him," he said.

27

"Here's a list of the bell times," he added, pointing to the page:

8:35 AM warning bell
8:40 AM short school assembly
8:50 AM roll call
9:00 AM Period 1
9:40 AM Period 2
10:40 AM Period 3
11:00—11:15 AM recess

"The bells are rung automatically by a timeclock, and I've checked it for accuracy," he continued. "Several people saw Pagett before the school assembly started, but so far, no one after it. Although all teachers are supposed to attend assemblies, not all of them do, and Pagett never did, so he wasn't seen from that point on."

"We know he didn't have a roll call. Who else was free in that ten minutes?" asked Carol.

"Here's a list of people who don't have to mark a class roll. Most of the teachers do have one, but the heads of departments are exempt, and, of the people we're interested in, Sybil Quade and Pete McIvor both miss out — she has extra duties coordinating senior work, and he teaches remedial reading two lunchtimes a week."

"Do we know the names of the teachers who actually attended the assembly before roll call?"

"I'm trying, but it's not easy — and anyone could slip away without being noticed."

"Come on, Mark, we've got to do better than this."

"Leaning on you, are they?" he asked sympathetically.

28

Carol sighed, thinking of the urgent telephone calls from the Commissioner of Police and from Sir Richard. "A bit," she said.

* * * * *

Sybil went to the last class of the day with a feeling of relief. It was a senior English class, and she wanted to sink into Shakespeare's language and forget the present. She smiled wryly to herself as she faced the class. After all, *Hamlet* was about death and suspicion, murder and motives, but somehow the familiar words in their iambic patterns seemed comforting.

Initially it was hard to keep the attention of the students — the events of the day before and the heat of the afternoon combined against her. But then began one of those lessons that sometimes spontaneously occur, where minds are caught and held. It was exhilarating and satisfying to be part of the comments, arguments, and insights bubbling in the class, and Sybil had no opportunity to think of anything else. When the final bell went she felt refreshed, smiling at the students as they hurried out of the room to the freedom of the hot summer afternoon.

"Can I speak to you for a minute?"

Sybil looked up at Evan's anxious face. He towered over her, gangling in that awkward half-boy, half-man stage. "What is it?"

"Catch you up," called Evan in response to a curious look from a friend who had paused in the doorway. He waited until they were alone, and then said, "Look, I didn't know who to ask. It's about Mr. Pagett."

Sybil stared at him. "Mr. Pagett?" she repeated stupidly.

Evan shifted nervously. "What I need to know is, well ... I want to know if I should go to the police."

"What about?"

"It's not important, really, but it might look. . . ." Evan paused, then said the rest in a rush. "The end of last week, after school, Mr. Pagett and I had a fight. It was about Hilary."

"Hilary Cosgrove?" asked Sybil, remembering that she hadn't been in the class sitting in her usual seat next to Evan.

Evan nodded miserably. "She's been seeing Mr. Pagett outside school. At his place. I didn't like it. I waited and caught him after lessons on Friday and asked him to stop seeing her, but he just laughed at me."

"Evan, why are you telling me this?"

"Because I punched him and knocked him over. I didn't mean to do it, but I lost my temper. And when I tried to say I was sorry, he yelled at me and said he'd make sure I failed my exams. Someone must have heard — the cleaners, someone. Do I go to the police and tell them, or do I wait and see if anyone else does?"

"You don't know anything about Mr. Pagett's death, do you?"

"No, of course not, but that's why. . . ." He shrugged, looking helpless.

Sybil felt a hypocrite as she said, "Then I think it would look better if you told them first. If someone already knows, they're going to find out anyway."

Evan ducked his head, embarrassed. "Thanks. Don't say anything about Hilary to anyone, will you?"

As Sybil watched him go she wondered if, under different circumstances, she would have taken the advice she had just given Evan, and told Carol Ashton the truth about seeing Bill. But what circumstances would let her willingly allow someone else to see her inner self? Her thoughts swung to Terry and the argument Carol Ashton had interrupted the day before. He wanted to possess her, to own her — not only physically, but mentally and emotionally. Terry had shouted at her, "I have every right to follow you, Syb. You know I love you. Tell me why you went to see Bill last night. I want to know." Carol Ashton ringing the front doorbell had cut into her furious reply.

She mechanically gathered her books together. "Greta Garbo was right," she said to the empty room, "I want to be alone."

Chapter Four

Sybil was sound asleep, dreaming that Carol Ashton's green eyes were appraising her coldly as Sybil was arrested for murder. The strident ring of the phone shattered the dream. Disoriented, she groped in the dark until she found the receiver. "Hello?"

Silence. She leaned to look at the clock. Ten past three. "Hello? Who's there? Tony, is that you?"

A whispered voice replied. "He woke up just as the drill went into his brain. He knew what was happening. I told him why he was dying."

She sat bolt upright, heart pounding. "Who is this? What are you saying?"

A whispered chuckle. "Syb. Syb, darling. You'll be next. A chain saw to cut off your pretty head. Don't interrupt. Listen. You're going to die and join Bill. You'd like that, wouldn't you? To lie with Bill?" A click, and then the burr of a disconnected line.

With a convulsive movement she turned on the light. Familiarity stared at her, somehow alien. Sybil looked at the phone, still in her hand, at the room, at the curtains moving lazily in the summer breeze.

Carol Ashton answered the telephone after five rings. She didn't sound sleepy or surprised. "Yes? Carol Ashton here."

"It's Syb."

"Pardon?"

"Sorry. It's Sybil Quade . . . the school. . . ."

"Of course. I didn't recognize your voice. What's happened?"

Carol listened without comment as Sybil repeated what she had heard. Then she said, "When you hang up, write down the whole message, fast. Will you do that?"

"Yes."

"The person actually threatened to cut off your head with a chain saw? In so many words?"

"Yes."

Carol assured her that it was probably a nuisance call, but she would arrange for a patrol car to search the house and surroundings. Was there anyone she could stay with for the rest of the night?

"I don't want to leave. I'll be all right."

Sybil was writing down every word she could remember when the telephone rang again. She stared at

33

it, and, after a moment of hesitation, picked up the receiver.

"Syb? Spoken to Inspector Ashton yet?" The same whisper. Could it be a woman? Sybil said nothing. "I know you're listening, Syb darling. Randy little bitch, you are. Deserve to lose your head. Is Carol Ashton coming round to comfort you, Syb? Maybe she'll make love to you. Would you like that? Make love fast, Syb. You haven't got long."

Sybil's hands were shaking as she dialed. Carol Ashton's line was engaged. Three times she tried until the cool voice answered. To herself, Sybil sounded almost casual. "Sorry to bother you again, but I've had another call from the same person."

"Write it down. Got a tape recorder? If you have, put it near the phone and try to record any other call you get." Carol's voice was reassuring. "Don't be frightened. A patrol car will be there soon, and I'll be about half an hour. Right? Ring someone to stay with you."

"What if the person I ask is the one making the calls?"

Carol gave a low laugh. "Good point. I'll see you soon."

Sybil dressed quickly. She felt somehow much better wearing clothes. She found herself looking for a weapon. Something to protect her, something to stop a chain saw. A vision of a poster for *The Texas Chain Saw Massacre* swam into her mind. She tried smoking again, and choked, as usual.

The uniformed police officers were reassuring. They searched each room and checked the garage and surroundings. "All clear," one of them said. "This has been the high point of our night. Shows what a boring job it is, eh?"

He broke off as Carol Ashton appeared at the doorway wearing jeans, a dark blue shirt and sneakers. He conferred with her for a moment, then both officers left.

"You're quite safe now. Let's get some coffee and go through the whole thing together."

They lounged opposite each other in comfortable chairs, Carol seeming younger and less severe in her causal clothes. She smiled across at Sybil. "They're upsetting, but a telephone call can't hurt you."

"I've got an unlisted number because of crank calls last year," said Sybil.

"Yes, I know. But of course, several people must have your number, so it wouldn't be impossible to find it out. It's on your personal information sheet, for example."

Sybil nodded. "I got the impression it wasn't a stranger."

"Can I see the messages?"

Sybil had written them on separate pieces of paper. Carol glanced at them, then asked her to read them aloud, as she had heard them. Sybil stumbled over the words of the second note, and looked up to meet Carol's green eyes. Sybil felt herself redden. She shrugged. "That's what he said."

"He? A whisper is basically sexless. Could it have been a woman?"

"Perhaps . . . I don't know. I just felt it was someone I knew — not a crank call — someone familiar." It was an appalling thought, that someone she knew well could be secretly smirking at her fear.

"Because the person called you Syb darling? Who would say that to you in ordinary conversation? Terry Clarke, for example?"

Sybil smothered a yawn, then stretched. "Terry never uses the term darling," she said with a faint smile.

Her smile disappeared as Carol said: "How about randy little bitch?"

Sybil met her gaze directly. "Terry has no reason at all to say that." She looked out at the dawn which was flooding the air with light and the liquid caroling of magpies.

"Has anyone else?"

The cold question shocked Sybil back into the reality of the situation. The lazy early morning light had seduced her into feeling secure. Now she sat upright, frighteningly conscious of why Carol Ashton sat opposite her, relaxed, cool, and waiting to trap her.

* * * * *

"Mrs. Dunstane?"

Florrie Dunstane looked up to meet Carol's friendly smile. The little, wispy, indeterminate woman smiled in return. "Yes, Inspector, can I help you?"

"Sorry to disturb you, as I know how busy you must be, but I wonder if you'd mind answering a few questions?"

Florrie Dunstane would be delighted. She followed the Inspector to the Principal's office with a thrill of anticipation. It was easy for people to ignore the administrative staff in a school, but Florrie had been at Bellwhether High for eleven years, first in the old dilapidated school, and then in the luxury of the modern buildings. The school community was an important part of her life: she followed with keen interest every rumor, every stray piece of gossip and indiscreet word. She had her favorites, and Bill Pagett had been one of them. Her pebble eyes darted around the office, imprinting every

36

detail for future regurgitation to Lionel, who waited patiently at home for her garrulous return.

"Your husband's an invalid," said Carol softly.

Florrie was impressed — this one had done her homework. Bourke watched with admiration as Carol's easy manner encouraged Florrie Dunstane's confidences to flow. Bill Pagett had been, she said, a "real charmer" with a smile and a word for the office staff every time he passed, always making a point of thanking them personally for anything they did for him, and often stopping for a joke or a comment about his colleagues or the students — not that it was gossip, of course.

"Mr. Pagett was interested in people, was he?" prompted Carol.

Florrie warmly agreed. She became expansive on the subject of the English staff. Did the police know that Alan Witcombe, the head of the English Department, was a religious nut who Bill had said would go bananas one day and kill someone? That Pete McIvor was in love with Antonia Waters from the Physical Education Department, but she threw him out and told Bill that he was just a boy trying to do a man's job? That Lynne Simpson was, well, not to put too fine a point on it, practically a nymphomaniac? Carol looked suitably surprised, asking if this was a generally held opinion. Florrie thought not. Bill knew things other people didn't.

"Did Bill Pagett himself have a relationship with Lynne Simpson?" asked Bourke, catching Carol's glance.

Florrie smiled. "Bill always said Lynne was too much for one man to handle, if you know what I mean, but they were always good friends. Lynne used to tell Bill all the problems she was having with Bruce. You know she's divorced? Well, Bill helped her through a really bad period, you know, giving her advice, fixing her up with a

37

good divorce lawyer so she wouldn't get cheated out of her rights. He was like that." She sniffed and dabbed at her eyes. "I can hardly believe he's gone."

Carol remembered how Lynne Simpson had waylaid her as she had walked with Mrs. Farrell to the staff meeting the morning of the murder. Mrs. Farrell had reluctantly introduced Lynne to her, ushering them into a vacant office for privacy while she pursued some administrative point with her deputy. "Inspector, I must tell you something important," Lynne had said, her hands clasped and her expression a nice mixture of regret and agitation. "This is in confidence, so please don't mention my name. It might have nothing to do with what's happened to Bill, but I think you should know Sybil Quade's marriage broke up because of him." Carol had asked a few pertinent questions, thanked her and watched her hurry off, wondering what had motivated her to volunteer the information.

"How does Lynne Simpson get on with Sybil Quade?" she asked Florrie.

Florrie showed no surprise at the question. "Wouldn't say they were close friends, but everything's all right. Actually, Lynne gets on with everyone, really, except Edwina Carter, but that's because Edwina's fat and Lynne's so attractive." Carol raised her eyebrows. "Jealousy," Florrie explained. "Edwina's nasty to Lynne, so she gives back what she gets."

"Did Bill Pagett mention anything about Sybil Quade's marriage?"

Yes, Bill had confided in her how regretful he was over the situation. He'd assured Florrie he hadn't meant to break up the marriage, but it was hardly his fault that Sybil had fallen in love with him. What made it worse was that Tony Quade was one of Bill's closest friends. It was

38

difficult, but Bill hoped he'd been fair to everyone. Florrie thought that he had.

"Did Tony Quade blame Bill Pagett for the failure of his marriage?" asked Carol.

"Blame Bill? Of course not. Why, after Sybil and Tony split up, Tony went to stay at Bill's place before he went back to England, and he wouldn't have done that if he'd blamed him, would he?"

Carol wanted to know if Florrie knew what Sybil Quade felt about the situation. Florrie shrugged. Sybil kept her feelings to herself. She was always nice and pleasant, but really, rather cold. You didn't know what she was thinking and she didn't share things the way Bill did. Florrie remembered Bill saying Sybil's problem was she was a bit frigid, wouldn't let herself go. That's why Bill said Terry Clark was wasting his time. It was an open secret Terry'd been keen on Sybil for ages, and he'd thought his chance had come when her husband left her, but Bill said he didn't have a hope.

"He didn't have a hope because she was in love with Bill Pagett?"

Florrie nodded. "That, too, as well as her being, well, not keen on that sort of thing."

Carol frowned. She asked if Sybil hadn't been keen on "that sort of thing" how was it she had fallen in love with Bill Pagett? Florrie could explain that. Bill was hard to resist, and even Sybil had succumbed to his charm.

Bourke interposed: "Did she actually have an affair with Mr. Pagett?"

Florrie said Bill had been too much of a gentleman to actually give any details, but she got the impression that Sybil had thrown herself at him, and he'd had to gently tell her it wasn't on.

39

"Did he mention any threats? Any emotional scenes?" asked Bourke.

Florrie shook her head. Bill wasn't the kind of person to repeat things like that — she'd just got the impression Sybil was awfully upset about the whole thing. More than that she couldn't say.

Carol wanted to know one other thing: had Florrie heard about anyone receiving anonymous telephone calls? Florrie was intrigued but unable to help. If there had been any such calls, she hadn't heard about them. Why, what was happening? Carol fielded the question, dismissing her with thanks.

"Sybil Quade looks promising," said Bourke after Florrie Dunstane had reluctantly departed.

"What's her motive?" asked Carol, irritated that she felt tempted to defend her. Be logical, she thought, and admit you don't want her guilty because she attracts you so much.

"The good old unrequited love, woman scorned etcetera," said Bourke. "She breaks up her marriage for love of Bill Pagett, and then he tells her to get lost. Of course, I'd rather our Sybil wasn't the one, so I favor Terry Clarke. Look at the situation from his point of view — Sybil's husband leaves the scene and he thinks he has her, then he discovers she's in love with Bill Pagett. That gives him a motive."

"Could be. I just wonder how reliable Florrie Dunstane's information is," said Carol.

"I think we know one thing," said Bourke, "Bill Pagett is shaping up to be a proper bastard."

"But such a charming one," said Carol.

* * * * *

40

The ceiling fans in the English staff room turned listlessly in the heat as Edwina, swathed in an extraordinary pink outfit, argued with Pete over the comparability of class grades. Sybil tried vainly to concentrate on essay marking. Usually lunchtime in the staff room was an oasis in a desert of lessons, but today the room was filled with irritable tension.

"Come on, Syb," said Terry, seizing her arm to pull her up from her desk, "a walk will do you good." She didn't resist as he steered her out the door. "Car park," he said shortly, "no kids there."

Sitting in Terry's red sports car, Sybil felt the first prick of real fear. Up to this point she had functioned automatically, viewing everything from a safe mental distance, but as she looked at Terry's hands, their backs covered with black hair, the fingers short and powerful, she could see them readying a power drill, tilting Bill's head forward, terminating his life.

"You didn't do it, did you Terry?"

He gave a snort of laughter. "Ah, Syb! You know I'd have broken his back with my bare hands. Power tools are too refined for me."

"Then who?"

He shrugged. "Who cares, as long as it doesn't touch us? Christ, there goes the bloody bell. Come on, Syb. Only three lessons to go."

As they walked together towards the English block he said, "Have any reporters bothered you at home?"

"A few have been camped out in the front of the house, but the Singletons behind me have let me park in their driveway and come in the back way. I can see from the front room who's at the door, and I've steadfastly ignored them when they've rung the bell. Anyway, I can't see why they'd bother to keep it up for long."

41

"They'll bother, Syb. It isn't every day the son of a famous ex-premier dies in such a satisfyingly bizarre way and of course they'll drag in all those oblique references to Sir Richard's questionable career and the current royal commission. The masses love it."

"I wouldn't be of any interest to anyone."

Terry was darkly amused. "No? You think that blonde bitch inspector won't dig up anything about the fascinating relationships between you, Tony and Bill? And she'd be an amateur compared to some of those bastards in the media." He stopped walking and swung her round to face him. "And you're so photogenic, Syb." She shrugged off his hands, but he seized her shoulders again. "Don't be such a fool, you need me to help you. Let me move in with you."

"No."

"When you change your mind, just ring me. I'll come right over."

"I won't change my mind," said Sybil.

* * * * *

Carol knocked on the front door of the substantial house, noting the BMW in the carport. Almost immediately the door was opened. "Mr. Berry?"

"Inspector, please come in."

He led her through to a luxurious lounge room, saying, "I'll get Evan for you. I want you to know I appreciate this, interviewing him here, at home. If possible, I'd like to keep it quiet. I know that might be asking a lot, but Evan hasn't done anything, really. He told me last night what had happened, so I stayed home with him today, expecting your call."

42

"You didn't consider it might be best to contact us yourself?"

"No one's withholding information," he blustered, "Evan can't really help you at all, I'm sure of that. He's just a kid."

Evan appeared, eyes downcast, awkward and embarrassed. "Sorry, I didn't do the right thing, did I? Should have seen you first. Mrs. Quade said to."

Carol opened her notebook. "You discussed it with Mrs. Quade?"

"Yesterday. She told me to tell first before you found out."

In looks the father was an older version of his son, but Evan's awkwardness had solidified in the father as uneasy belligerence. "Look, Inspector, I've been in touch with my solicitors. I wanted someone here to protect Evan's rights, but I was persuaded it wasn't necessary."

"There's no thought of Evan being charged with anything, Mr. Berry."

"No. Of course there isn't. He hasn't done anything wrong. Argued with a teacher, that's all."

Turn the charm up a notch, thought Carol. "Mr. Berry, I know how concerned you must feel, but any information about Mr. Pagett could be important, not by itself, but as part of the overall investigation."

Berry nodded a reluctant assent, watching narrowly as Carol smiled at Evan and said, "I'd just like you to tell me about Mr. Pagett. Did you know him well?"

"Not personally, no."

"But you knew things about him?"

"Oh, yes. Everyone knows how he chats up the girls at school. Being a teacher, he's not supposed to, but he's gone out with lots of them."

Carol asked a few gentle questions. Her dislike of Bill Pagett grew as she listened to Evan's stumbling answers about a teacher who had quite plainly abused his position to gain sexual favors.

"This is disgusting!" Evan's father was red-faced. "What's being done about this sort of thing?" He glared at his son. "You should have told me."

"And what would you have done, Dad? Rushed down to the school with a shotgun?"

Carol intervened. "Could we discuss the argument you had with Mr. Pagett last Friday afternoon?"

Evan licked his lips and took a deep breath. "It was about Hilary Cosgrove. She's a girl in my year . . . we've been friends all through school. When she started to get keen on Mr. Pagett I tried to warn her, but she wouldn't listen —"

His father interrupted. "You should have told me. I'd have gone to her father and straightened the whole mess out."

Carol nodded to him sympathetically, hiding her irritation, and said to Evan, "So you approached Mr. Pagett direct?"

"Well, Hilary wouldn't listen to me. She knew he'd been with lots of other girls at school, but she said he was different with her, that he really loved her. . . ."

"Oh, yes!" said Mr. Berry bitterly.

Carol ignored the interruption. "You argued with him over Hilary?"

"It was after school. Everyone had gone, and I caught him leaving the staff room last. He wouldn't listen to me, and I lost my temper and hit him."

"Evan's only a boy, Inspector! He's not violent, never has been. Just acts before he thinks. Doesn't mean anything."

Carol gave the father another placatory nod, then looked encouragingly at Evan. "What happened when you hit him?"

"He fell down. It was a lucky punch — he just lost his balance and ended up on the ground." He looked at his dangling hands. "See? I bruised my knuckles."

"You hit him with your right hand?"

"Yes. I didn't want a fight, really I didn't. Tried to say I was sorry, but he yelled at me. Said he'd make sure Hilary never spoke to me again. Said he'd make sure I'd fail my exams."

"All this while lying on the ground?"

Evan smiled faintly. "All this while getting up. And then he took a swing at me, but I dodged him. It was no good trying to speak to him, so I left."

"He didn't try to chase you?"

"No. Just kept shouting."

Carol asked a few more questions, noted the names of school girls Evan thought had been out with Pagett, soothed Mr. Berry's ruffled feathers, and went thoughtfully back to Bellwhether High.

Bourke wasn't in the office, but he had left two messages on the desk. She sighed when she saw she was to ring Sir Richard urgently, and frowned over the second one: *Edwina Carter says she got a mystery call last night. Won't speak to anyone but you. Said you'd be back about two.*

There was also a preliminary lab report on Bill Pagett's woodwork room. Nothing helpful with the fingerprints, but that was to be expected; a confirmation that nothing in the room had hair or skin fragments to indicate it had been used as a weapon to knock Pagett unconscious; an analysis of matter vacuumed up from the murder scene — sawdust, of course; fragments of wood

45

and metal; dried flakes of shellac and colored lacquer; the expected dust, dirt and vegetable matter tramped in by students' feet.

Bourke had also placed a neat table on the desk. As she studied it, Carol sipped an orange juice he had thoughtfully left for her. She looked first at the entries of particular interest:

PAGETT DIES BETWEEN 8:40–9:10

	ASSEMBLY 8:40–8:50	ROLL CALL 8:50–9:00	START PERIOD 1 9:00–9:10
CLARKE, Terry	present (confirmed)	class 10.3 (marked roll)	free — was taking car to garage for servicing
CARTER, Edwina	absent — booking video	class 7.4 (marked roll)	11EC watching video Room A5
McIVOR, Pete	present (?)	no roll class	11EM Room A3
QUADE, Sybil	spoke at start — then?	no roll class	free period
QUADE, Tony	whereabouts not known but Commonwealth Bank confirms his bankcard used to withdraw cash from automatic teller, Collins Street, Melbourne last Sunday at 10:32 AM		
SIMPSON, Lynne	present (confirmed)	class 7.7 (marked roll)	11ES in library (NB she's usually late to class)
WITCOMBE, Alan	present (confirmed)	no roll	free period

At the bottom he had added in pencil: *Evan Berry late to school on Monday — had to put name in late book in front office — time noted as 9:15 AM.*

46

Carol was absently rolling a pen between her fingers when Bourke came back to the office. "Hi, how'd you go with the kid?"

Carol gave him a brief outline of the interview. He made a face over the father's reaction to Bill Pagett's activities. "Hell, Carol, you seen the girls round here? They look a million dollars and they're not kids, you know. I can understand how Pagett felt." He caught her look and grinned. "Not that I think he should have done anything about it, of course."

"Is there anything new?" said Carol to change the subject.

"You saw the messages? Edwina Carter is agog with some information, but she wouldn't trust me at all. I used my boyish charm, too."

"No wonder she clammed up."

"And there's a letter for you marked urgent and personal." He placed it carefully on the desk. "I've got a feeling about it. Don't think it's the usual crank mail."

Carol examined the envelope. "When did it arrive?"

"The mail this morning, sent care of the school. Posted yesterday at the local post office, so there was no delay in getting it. Sat in the office until now when Florrie Dunstane stirred herself to give it to me. Probably been busy steaming it open."

Carol slit the envelope carefully. Her name, title and the school address were printed neatly in sloping block capitals. The sheet of paper inside was creased in several places, and had been refolded to fit the envelope exactly. "Interesting," she said as she saw the signature, "not a common name."

Bourke leaned over her shoulder. "Well, Sybil Quade strikes again," he said. "I wonder who was thoughtful

47

enough to send us this? There's no helpful little return address on the envelope, is there?"

"You know there isn't," said Carol. "This looks like a note from Sybil Quade to Bill Pagett."

"And so intense," said Bourke, reading it. "Ah, redheads! Fiery little things they are! Even I might kill for Sybil Quade."

"Sybil Quade might kill for herself," said Carol. "Take a couple of photocopies, will you, and send the envelope and letter in for examination."

Edwina's bright pink clothing appeared in the doorway. She beamed at Carol. "Inspector, you're back. I don't suppose your off-sider here told you I wanted to see you urgently?"

"I was just about to contact you."

"Well, I've saved you the trouble."

As Edwina settled herself in a chair, Carol was struck by her tidy movements. Large though she was, she moved with an almost graceful economy. She had small, neat feet and hands, and her curly hair and pretty face could have belonged to a huge baby. An enthusiastic baby, thought Carol, as Edwina fixed her with a bright gaze, the pink of her clothes reflecting against her already flushed face.

"This could be nothing, but I thought you should know," Edwina said with satisfaction. Bourke flipped open his notebook as she continued, "It was about two-thirty this morning. The phone rang and I got up to answer it. Thought it could have been a student making a nuisance call, although kids usually make them later in the year when they've managed to work up a few good healthy grudges against teachers. Anyhow, I picked up the phone to hear a whispering voice threatening me."

"Did you recognize the person?"

48

Edwina looked at Bourke with scorn. "All whispers sound pretty much the same. I couldn't even tell if it was a man or woman but I'm pretty sure it wasn't a kid."

"Can you remember exactly what was said?" asked Carol, leaning forward, intrigued by Edwina's calm attitude.

"It was fairly close to this: I say hello. The whisper says 'Fat Eddy, darling' so I ask who it is, and the voice says 'Fat Eddy Carter bouncing down the cliff. What a splatter you'll make at the bottom.' Of course, this makes me angry, so I ask who the hell it is again, and the line goes dead."

Bourke looked up from his notebook. "Is that all?"

"No. I'm halfway back to bed when the phone rings again. I pick it up and the same voice says 'Fat Eddy Carter, falling down the cliff. Exploding like a bag of lard on the rocks. What a mess.' Then whoever it is hangs up."

"Did you get the impression the call was just meant to frighten you, or do you think you're in some personal danger?" said Carol.

Edwina gestured with spread hands. "Who knows? Before Bill's death I would have said it was just some tacky little pervert getting a sick thrill, but now...."

"Have you ever had a call like this before?" asked Bourke.

"No. I've had kids ringing up with obscenities, and even *I* have had the odd heavy-breather, but up till now no one's ever suggested I bounce down a cliff face."

"Do you have any idea who it might be? I'm not asking for evidence, but just your instincts."

Edwina beamed at her. "I know who I'd like it to be — my dear colleague, Lynne Simpson. Unfortunately I can't, in good conscience, blame Lynne because she has at least one good quality — she stabs you in the front, rather than

49

the back. It would be quite out of character for her to make an anonymous phone call. She's such an egoist she couldn't bear not to be identified immediately." She became reflective. "Inspector, I suppose you know about Lynne and Bill?"

"Could you explain?"

"Well, of course it's just gossip, but Lynne was rather keen on Bill, but he lost interest in her fairly fast. I think he liked them younger, and more pliant."

Edwina left in good humor, amused at the arrangements to have her telephone monitored and brushing aside any suggestions that she might be in serious danger. "I never go near cliffs," she said as a parting line.

Carol and Bourke sat looking at each other. "Well," said Bourke, "I can think of four possibilities: one, it's the same person who rang Sybil Quade, and who may or may not be the murderer; two, it's a straight-out pervert who's got nothing to do with the other calls or the murder; three, it's Sybil Quade, who pretends to get two threatening messages so she won't be suspected when she rings Edwina; four, Edwina's jealous that Sybil's getting interesting telephone calls, so she makes one up for herself."

"Does Edwina know about Sybil's anonymous calls? I asked her not to tell anyone, and as far as I'm aware, she hasn't."

Bourke shrugged. "Search me. I don't know who Sybil whispers her little secrets to, although I'd volunteer to listen if she gave me the chance."

"Why do you think the calls, if they do exist, are being made at all?"

"It might appeal to the kind of person who gets a charge out of drilling a hole in someone's head," said

Bourke, "or, for that matter, someone who just likes to cause trouble and settle old scores with a few whispered threats." He flicked a forefinger at a printed Bellwhether High staff list. "Probably someone here. Pity Telecom are so inefficient, or we'd be able to trace the calls. What do you think our chances are of having the phones tapped? A voice print would be nice."

Carol shook her head. "I don't think there'll be any more . . . the person isn't a fool, and would know it might be getting dangerous. Besides, we'd have a hell of a time getting a court order — things are very sensitive after the last scandal about illegal phone tapping."

"Even with Sir Richard's influence?"

"Especially with Sir Richard's influence. You've obviously forgotten the royal commission's considering transcripts of an illegal tap on *his* phone."

Bourke looked impatient. "So what about Sybil Quade? She's still got a tape recorder on the line."

"Yes, but I doubt if anything of use will come from it. And if she is the person making the calls, she'll just turn it off before she dials." She handed him the lab report. "Have you read this? I want more details on the stuff they vacuumed up from the floor and desk. I want to know exactly what was there."

"How much detail?" said Bourke, still irritated. "Do you want the Latin name of a leaf that blew in from the playground?"

"I do."

The phone interrupted them. She left Bourke to answer it, and pulled the curtain back to gaze out at the deserted playgrounds. The pulse of the school was determined by bells: students and teachers alike ebbed and flowed at their strident commands. Now all was peaceful, the noise and movement of lunchtime replaced

51

by a muted hum from classrooms. A dog inspected the overflowing dustbins, one or two students dawdled along on some message, and Mrs. Farrell sailed by on her afternoon inspection of her domain.

"Just amazing," said Bourke, slamming down the phone. "You'll just never guess what the science guys have found." He shook his head. "Amazing," he repeated.

"Are you going to tell me, or do I use my psychic powers?"

"Sorry. It's a power drill they tested from Sybil Quade's garage. The drill bit showed positive for blood and tissue."

"But the murder weapon was definitely the Black and Decker by the body."

"Oh, it's not human. The analysis shows fragments of lamb bone and tissue. Looks like she made a practice run to see how easy it would be to drill into human bone."

Carol said nothing, her vivid imagination casting up an image of Sybil, her red head bent in concentration as she experimented with a power drill and a leg of lamb.

Bourke broke into her thoughts. "And there were a couple of her fingerprints on the body of the drill. I'm dying to see how she explains this away."

"So am I," said Carol.

* * * * *

Mrs. Farrell answered the phone to Sir Richard's warm tones, surprised by the speed with which he had replied to her earlier message. "Phyllis? You have something for me?"

"I don't know, Sir Richard. It's really only gossip. So hard to decide if there's any substance to it, and I don't want to distress you with rumors. . . ."

52

"Anything about my son that could help solve his murder is important to me. Of course I realize that rumors may have no foundation, but there may be a grain of truth, something that will help me, and, of course, the police. Please tell me all you know, however trivial."

Never having been deeply interested in others' personal lives and petty scandals, Mrs. Farrell found the gathering of gossip distasteful, but surprisingly easy. In a businesslike tone she itemized the details for Sir Richard; he listened silently. In essence, there were three main points: first, it was said Bill Pagett had a regrettable tendency to form short-term relationships with senior girls in the school — and if Mrs. Farrell had known about this, she added, she would, of course, have acted to stop it immediately. She didn't repeat the words of one anonymous letter: 'Pagett's going through Bellwhether's senior girls like a hot knife through butter.' Second, he was credited with breaking up the marriage of one of his colleagues on the English staff. Her name was Sybil Quade. Mrs. Farrell had not, of course, spoken to her personally. Third, he had recently had a violent confrontation with the head of the English Department, Alan Witcombe.

"What exactly was the argument about?" asked Sir Richard.

Mrs. Farrell sighed to herself. "I must tell you, Sir Richard, that it gives me no pleasure to discuss the private concerns of any staff member. Suffice it to say that Mr. Witcombe and your son were diametrically opposed on moral and religious grounds."

Sir Richard wanted more details, and with distaste Mrs. Farrell gave a judicious selection, terminating the call with promises to contact him if anything else came up.

Half an hour later, Sir Richard was back on the phone. Mrs. Farrell was impressed by the evidence of his influence on the usually obdurate Education Department and irritated by his aggrieved tone. "Phyllis, I'm sorry to find you haven't been absolutely frank with me. I can't believe you didn't know that Alan Witcombe was removed from his last school because of a scandal."

"It's rather an exaggeration to call it a scandal, Sir Richard. The Education Department decided it would be better for all concerned if Mr. Witcombe took another appointment. It was merely some type of minor interpersonal conflict, and surely not relevant to the present situation."

"Not relevant? That he physically threatened not only several students, but parents also?"

Mrs. Farrell felt an unaccustomed desire to raise her voice, but resisted to say in a neutral tone, "To be precise, Mr. Witcombe stated the students should be horsewhipped after he found them in what, to him, was a highly compromising situation outside a school dance."

"I'm extremely surprised, Phyllis, that you have failed to see how important this is. The man is obviously some sort of religious extremist and his argument with Bill was based on his fanatical ideas about religion and morals. Does Inspector Ashton know about this?"

Mrs. Farrell said that the Departmental records had been given to the police, and yes, she would check with the Inspector immediately to make sure Alan Witcombe's past indiscretions had been noted. She pursed her lips as she carefully replaced the receiver after Sir Richard's cold farewell. Just how cooperative did the Education Department expect her to be?

* * * * *

54

"Syb."

Sybil looked up from the school library catalog at Lynne's urgent tone. Although Lynne managed to inject drama into every situation, this time she looked genuinely disturbed. "Syb, you've only got a junior class. Can they look after themselves for a minute? It's rather urgent I talk to you, privately."

The junior students showed fluctuating enthusiasm for the library research assignment Sybil had set them, but the librarian volunteered to keep an eye on their endeavors, so she followed Lynne into the empty senior studies room.

Shutting the door, Lynne said, "Have you heard from Tony?"

Sybil stiffened. "Why would I?" she asked.

"You know he's in Australia, don't you?"

"The police told me. How do you know?"

Lynne flung herself down in a chair. "Syb, you're not going to like this." She looked up at Sybil's blank face. "Bill told me Tony was coming back. The fact is, Tony was supposed to be staying at Bill's place from Sunday onwards. He was flying up from Melbourne."

Sybil stared at her. Had Tony been there while she and Bill had screamed at each other? Suddenly she felt physically sick as she struggled to concentrate on Lynne, who was still speaking.

"But Tony turned up at my place late Sunday night. Told me he and Bill had just had a violent row — about you, Syb."

Sybil thought of the whispered threats on the phone. She said firmly, "I haven't seen Tony or heard from him. Where is he now?"

"That's why I had to speak to you. I don't know what to do. Tony stayed Sunday night with me. No one else knows — Bruce had the kids for the weekend so we were alone. He's still got them, actually. I couldn't face having them around when it might be dangerous. Anyway, early on Monday Tony said he was going to have it out with Bill. I haven't seen him since. Thought he might have been in touch with you."

Sybil shook her head as Lynne stared intensely at her. Lynne said urgently: "Because you see what it means, don't you Syb? Tony could be the one who killed Bill."

"I don't believe it."

"Syb! *I* don't want to believe it either! But look at the facts: Tony quarrels with Bill, leaves me early on Monday, the day Bill is murdered, and disappears. Where is he? Why hasn't he contacted someone?"

"Have you told the police?"

"Not yet. I was hoping . . . well, I thought you should know first, anyway." Lynne stood, looking indecisive, then she said in a rush, "Syb, be careful, won't you? Of Tony, I mean. If he did kill Bill, then you were the reason."

* * * * *

"I'm sorry to keep you back after school," said Carol to Terry Clarke, who sat, arms folded, glaring at her. "It's about your movements on Monday morning."

"Look, I've answered all these questions for this guy," he said, jerking his head to indicate Bourke, "so why do I have to go through them again?"

"In your statement you say that you left the school immediately after roll call on Monday to deliver your car to a garage for servicing."

56

"So?"

"Someone claims to have seen you near the administration block at the time you say you were outside the school grounds."

Terry settled back in the chair, frowning. "Someone's mistaken, or lying."

His eyes swung to meet Bourke's question: "Why didn't you drop your car off earlier? Coming here first meant you had to double back, since you passed the service station on the way to school."

Terry was offhand. "I was late. I didn't have time. Farrell raises hell if you don't sign the attendance book before school. She actually rules it off and stands there, daring anyone who's late to front her." He looked back at Carol. "Okay? Satisfied?" His frown deepened at her noncommittal expression. "Look, Inspector, I didn't kill Pagett and I don't know who did. Anyone who says they saw me is wrong. Now, can I go?"

Carol played with a pen. "It's been suggested to us that you were jealous of Mr. Pagett's relationship with Sybil Quade."

Terry laughed scornfully. "Jesus! You'd listen to anyone, wouldn't you?"

"That's our job," said Bourke.

Terry unfolded his arms and leaned across the desk.

Carol resisted the impulse to move back, and met him eye to eye.

"Look," he said, "I get the impression you're trying to pin this on Syb. Don't waste your time. As far as Pagett's concerned, she feels the same as I do — wouldn't spit on the bastard if he was dying of thirst in a desert — but wouldn't murder him, either. Pagett wouldn't be worth doing time for."

57

After he had stalked out, Bourke said, "That one would bash you to death. He wouldn't bother using a drill. You know he does weights every afternoon?"

"Yes, and he belongs to a rifle club, but Bill Pagett wasn't shot."

Bourke turned his hands palms up. "I bow to your superior logic," he said, "so tell me why Clarke finds it necessary to have Sybil spitting in a desert."

Carol laughed at his words, then grew thoughtful. "Terry Clarke seems keen to protect Mrs. Quade, but maybe he's just trying to make sure we don't overlook her," she said.

"Subtle," said Bourke, "and for my money, too refined for him to even think of. If you ask me, I think it's Terry and our Syb in it together."

"What makes you think that?"

"Well, it makes sense. Sybil's the brain who sets it up, and Terry's the brawn who carries it out."

"Terry Clarke has an M.A. in English Lit from Sydney University," said Carol, "so I think you'd better consider the possibility that along with the brawn he has the brains."

She smiled at his expression. "I've arranged for a female police officer to accompany you to interview Hilary Cosgrove," she said. "I'll see Mrs. Quade."

"Swap you," said Bourke. "You take the kid and I'll take the delectable Syb. No? Ah, well, she'd probably fool me, anyway." He shuffled through papers on the desk. "Look, before I go, have a look at this." He handed her one of his neat pages. "You asked me to find out if anyone had special medical expertise to help them drill the hole in Pagett's head. That's all I've got."

He left Carol frowning at the page. Terry Clarke's interest in martial arts might give him some detailed

58

knowledge of anatomy; Edwina's father had been a dentist (Bourke had written "far-fetched, but after all, concentrating on the head!"); both Pete McIvor and Sybil had advanced first aid qualifications; but for Lynne Simpson and Alan Witcombe he could find nothing of interest. He was still waiting for information on Tony Quade from England.

Carol sat thinking long after the last sounds of activity had faded and the school became strangely quiet. She rested her chin on her linked fingers and stared unseeingly out the door and down the silent corridor.

Lynne Simpson had made a dramatic entrance just before Terry Clarke had arrived, breathless with her news of Tony Quade and full of insincere apologies for keeping the information to herself for three days. "One's loyalty to one's friends," she said soulfully, "that's the only explanation I can give."

Carol resisted the tart remark that rose to her tongue and listened with flattering attention to Lynne's story. "I've told Syb," Lynne concluded, "though I suppose you'll say I shouldn't have. Anyway, I'm sure she's seen Tony, though she says she hasn't."

Neat knife job, thought Carol, I wonder if she has a grudge against Sybil as well as Edwina? As Lynne turned to go, Carol remarked, "We've been told you and Bill Pagett were rather more than friends at one time." To Lynne's look of inquiry, she added, "But that he lost interest, and switched to someone younger."

Lynne's lips had twitched. "Oh, dear," she had said, "I do hope Edwina isn't leading you up the garden path. She has *such* an active imagination."

Carol's thoughts now strayed to Tony Quade. She had a photograph of him, but it was difficult to read character into the regular features that gazed out at her. She found herself actively hoping that Sybil's husband was guilty. Even so, Sybil would have to endure probing questions and the curious gaze of strangers into her personal affairs, but at least she would not be charged, and consigned to the cold brutality of a women's prison. Her gaze dropped to the photostat of Sybil's note. Who had sent it, and why? Had the power drill been planted to incriminate her too? She gave herself a mental shake. She was acting as though she was on Sybil's side, and, of course, she wasn't. "My only interest is the truth," she said mockingly to the silent office.

She checked a file and dialed a number. "Mrs. Quade? It's Carol Ashton here. I hope this isn't inconvenient, but I wonder if I could call by and see you, now? In about twenty minutes, then."

Carol didn't get up immediately, re-reading the short note and picturing Sybil's face as she wrote it. It was undated, and the angular writing hurried urgently across the paper:

Bill,

I won't say anything to Tony about what happened, so you don't have to make up any convincing lies. I don't ever want to think about it again.

Sybil

She packed her briefcase slowly, uncomfortably aware of how much she was looking forward to seeing Sybil again. Straight women, she thought bitterly. You know where that leads — and it isn't worth it.

* * * * *

60

As Carol walked up the steps, Sybil, who had changed to shorts and a brief top, opened the door. Smiling, she said, "Your call just caught me — I was going for a swim." She added impulsively, "Have you got a costume with you in the car? Do you want to come with me?"

"I'm sorry — no. I'll only keep you a short time."

Carol watched Sybil take the photostat and read it. The animation in her face was suddenly stilled. She didn't look up immediately, but reread the words. She's not going to tell the truth, thought Carol.

Sybil handed the photostat back. "It's nothing, really. Bill and I had some stupid disagreement over something. I can't even remember what it was, now. Anyway, I wrote him a note because Tony hated it if we didn't get along — his best friend and his wife — and I didn't want Bill to mention it."

"Rather an intense note for a friendly disagreement," said Carol.

"Perhaps I express myself badly."

Carol smiled at her. "Somehow I doubt that. You can't be any more explicit?"

"No." Sybil was self-possessed. She raised her eyebrows. "I do hope, Inspector, you haven't been pinning too much on this note. It really was of no importance."

"You haven't asked me how I came to have it, Mrs. Quade."

Sybil looked surprised. "Why, I imagine you found it at Bill's place. It's the sort of thing he'd do — keep a stupid little letter like that."

"We didn't find it there. Someone posted it to me, anonymously."

Carol watched Sybil's face tighten.

"Who would do that?" Sybil said.

"I was hoping you could tell me that."

61

Sybil suddenly became brisk. "No, I'm sorry. Now, if there's nothing else. . . ."

"Do you do your own repairs around the home?"

"What?"

"Are you familiar with the use of common power tools, for example?"

"Anyone can plug in a Black and Decker and use it — that's what you mean, isn't it?"

"Have you ever used any of the power tools in the Industrial Arts Department?"

"Of course I haven't. What are you getting at?"

"You had a power drill on the bench in your garage. You gave permission for it to be taken for tests."

"Tests?"

"The drill bit itself had small pieces of flesh and bone clinging to it." At Sybil's appalled expression she added, "It wasn't human. The forensic department says it's animal matter, lamb to be exact."

"You mean someone was . . . practicing?" She stared at Carol. "*Here*?"

Oh, very good, thought Carol — either you're bright, or guilty, or both. Aloud she said, "A trial run. I don't suppose you have any other explanation?" Sybil shook her head. "Has anyone borrowed your power drill lately?"

"I loaned it to Pete a week or so ago. His flat had been burgled and he wanted to install safety locks on the windows. He gave it back to me last Friday, I put it on the front seat of the car, and when I drove in I left it on the bench."

"Was there a drill bit in it?"

"No, Pete gave me back the bits in their separate plastic case."

"Is the garage kept locked?"

Sybil sounded defeated. "No."

"So anyone could come in?"

"Anyone," said Sybil wearily. "Are you finished?"

"I'd like you to show me the garage, and also I'd like your permission for a closer scientific examination of the area. Will that be all right?"

Sybil was white, but self-contained. "Why would I be so stupid as to leave evidence like that on a drill?" she said.

Carol thought, Because of monstrous self-confidence, or nerves, or just an oversight. Aloud she said, "I can't speculate on that."

"Inspector, do you think I need legal representation?"

"That must be your decision."

"I wish I knew what you were really thinking," said Sybil, turning to lead the way to the garage.

No, you don't, thought Carol, watching the graceful turn of her head.

Chapter Five

Carol was cleaning her teeth when the telephone rang.
She glanced at her watch. Seven o'clock on a burnished
summer morning. "Yes? Carol Ashton. What?"

She listened intently. "Right. Put a clamp on this. No
news, especially radio stations. I'll be there as soon as I
can."

She rang Mark Bourke. "Mark? You heard?
Extraordinary in light of the phone call to Edwina Carter,
isn't it? And I don't want Sybil Quade to know anything

before I speak to her. I'll leave that side to you. I'm going down to the beach."

Even though Carol had changed into jeans and jogging shoes she found it difficult to clamber around the rocks at the base of the headland. It was just after eight, but the day was already singing with heat, the light shattering on the heaving water and splintering into her eyes. "Much further?" she asked the young constable.

"No, Inspector. Just round this rock fall." Carol looked up at the overhang. "Quite a recent one," said the constable helpfully. "The rock's rotten. Look, there's where the next lot's going to go. See the crack?"

"You're a comfort," said Carol, laughing.

The body was near Carter's Cave, which was actually a huge cleft in the cliff face. Its floor was composed of earth, stones and debris that had fallen from above, the walls narrowing at the top to allow further debris to form the roof. Below the cave a rock platform covered with jumbled sandstone blocks stretched to the sea. The tidal pools glittered in the sunlight and the dull thump and suck of the water added a continuous accompaniment. Carol looked up to the top of the cliff where several uniformed figures stood, curious onlookers. "He fell from up there?"

"Looks like it," said the constable. "Otherwise he wouldn't have landed where he did, just above the high water mark." He pointed to where a group of men in white overalls stood patiently waiting for the photographer to finish, for Carol to view the body and for the basket stretcher to bump its way to the top with its dead burden.

Tony Quade lay in a curious position, face down, one knee drawn up under him, his hands outstretched as if paying homage to some greater power. "There was a passport in his pocket," said the constable. "This kid found him about six this morning. As soon as we realized who it was, you were contacted."

Carol walked over to the white-faced boy, who was staring with sick fascination at the activity around the body. She put a hand on his shoulder and turned him away towards the sea. "Tell me how you found him," she said.

The boy swallowed. "I came down to fish," he said, a tremor in his voice. "Climbed down from up there. I was almost at the bottom when I saw him. Just lying like that. I came up close. Told myself he was asleep, but knew he wasn't, really. I could see the blood. I watched for ages to see if he was breathing." He looked up at Carol. "You know, I was frightened he might be alive . . . that he might turn over and his face would be all smashed. . . ."

Carol asked a few more quiet questions, then sent the boy off with the constable to make a written statement. The tide was licking closer, but the water would only wash within a few feet of the outstretched broken hands. High water was at 8:48 AM and it was 8:30 now. "Turn him over," she said.

The photographer, chewing gum relentlessly, clicked away with bored competence, unaffected by the smashed face and congealed blood that once had been the handsome Tony Quade. He shifted the gum to his other cheek. "These jumpers," he muttered.

"This one had a lot to live for," said Carol, thinking of Sybil's red hair — and of her mouth. "And not much to die for. I don't think it's suicide. I want everything on this, fast."

* * * * *

66

Carol went straight into the office without changing from her jeans. She caught Bourke's slight confirming nod that he thought Sybil had been isolated from the news of her husband's death.

Sybil was sitting tautly, an untouched cup of coffee on the table beside her. "What's happened? Why am I being kept here?"

Carol didn't answer immediately, but walked deliberately around Mrs. Farrell's polished desk to sit with the light behind her. Did Sybil already know what was about to be said because she had pushed her husband to his death? A vivid picture, clear as a movie, danced in her imagination: Tony Quade meeting his estranged wife, arguing with her, turning his back in contempt, and then, the impulsive shove, the body turning, the scream blending with the shrieks of wheeling seagulls.

"Did you see or speak to anyone last night?" asked Bourke mildly.

"Why?" She sighed. "You won't answer, will you? All right. Inspector Ashton saw me late yesterday afternoon. After she'd gone I drank about half a bottle of whiskey, all alone. I rang a friend who's moved up the coast and told her what had happened. Then I cried myself to sleep. Okay? Is that what you want? Now, why?"

Carol said with brutal directness, "I've just come from examining a body. We believe it is your husband. He fell, or was pushed, to his death."

Sybil said nothing, merely covering her eyes with one hand. Carol wondered if it was to hide grief, fear, or exultation. Bourke raised his eyebrows to Carol in an unspoken question. At her silent assent he pulled up a chair and sat directly in front of Sybil.

67

"I know what a shock this must have been," he said sympathetically. "Would you like a glass of water or a fresh cup of coffee?"

She takes shock so well, thought Carol, or is it arrogance that gives her that iron control? Carol didn't interrupt Bourke as he was by turns solicitous, concerned, and cajoling in an effort to get Sybil to react, to talk, even to cry. She seemed remote, answering his questions politely, but asking none of her own.

Finally Bourke said, "You don't seem very interested in the details, Mrs. Quade."

"You mean that under the circumstances I don't seem to be acting appropriately?" said Sybil bitterly.

"There are many different reactions," said Bourke soothingly.

"Oh? Perhaps I'd better start playing my role more effectively, or else you'll be sure I'm guilty, won't you?"

"Of what?" said Bourke carefully.

Sybil was openly scornful. "Why, of murdering my estranged husband."

"We didn't mention murder. It might simply be an accident, or perhaps he took his own life. . . ." Bourke let the sentence trail away suggestively.

"Suicide? Tony suicide? You've got to be joking."

Bourke's voice was pitched to show regretful sincerity. "Mrs. Quade, we have to consider every possibility. For example, one scenario could be that your husband murdered Bill Pagett, and then, after brooding for a couple of days, killed himself."

"Did Tony leave a note?"

Did she hate him? thought Carol. How can she be so cold?

"We haven't found one," said Bourke, "but that doesn't mean there isn't a note."

"Can I go?" asked Sybil. "I have classes to cover."

"Mrs. Quade," said Carol as she reached the door. Sybil looked back at her. "I'm sorry to make this request, but you will need to make an identification of the body."

"When?"

"As soon as possible. I'll make the arrangements and inform you."

Sybil nodded, then said, "Will you take me?"

"Of course," said Carol.

* * * * *

Mrs. Farrell felt besieged. The discovery of Tony Quade's body had revitalized the corps of reporters who had clustered around the school entrances since Bill Pagett's death. She had run the gauntlet as she entered the school car park, resisting the unaccustomed temptation to mow down a shrill television personality. As it was, she had accidentally nudged the woman with the front of her car, a move that met with a howl of protest from the victim and the clicking of cameras from the rest. Now the Minister had instructed her to make a statement, and was sending a trusted representative to help her frame it.

As she juggled with the preliminary outline, conscious that she had to project the correct image, say the correct things and basically give little, if any, information, one of the office staff brought in her mail. She sorted through it rapidly. Her hands suddenly stilled as she came upon a plain square envelope addressed in sloping printed. capitals and marked 'personal and private.' It was identical to the ones she had been receiving, and destroying, over the past few months.

She turned it in her hands. Destroy it unread? Give it to the Inspector? To Sir Richard? Slowly she slit it open.

* * * * *

They drove in silence, Sybil imagining an invisible string pulling the car towards the hideous thing waiting in a refrigerated cocoon for her to say, yes, I think that's Tony. What would he look like? She took a deep breath.

Carol glanced at her. "You okay?"

"Yes." Sybil turned resolutely to the beaches that unwound beneath the coast road. If only she was one of those distant figures lounging on the sand, lazily watching the Pacific lick the shore, concerned merely with the darkness of a tan. She took another deep breath, looking at Carol's calm profile. "How do people usually behave when they . . . when they see someone's body?" she asked. "I'm not sure what I'm asking . . . how long do I have to stay. . . ."

The green eyes considered her for a moment before returning to the road. "Only a short time. It will help you to just keep one thing in mind — to identify the person. Don't think what happened, or about the past or future — just give yourself one task to accomplish, and ignore everything else."

"Will you be there?"

"Of course. And don't worry about fainting, or anything like that. It'll all be over in a few moments." Hearing her own soothing words, Carol felt like a hypocrite. She knew what Sybil was about to see: a person she remembered as vital and alive was now dead meat on a slab. She tried to see the smashed flesh, broken bones, dried blood through Sybil's eyes. "Try to think about something else," she said, knowing it was futile advice.

70

After they left the beaches, the traffic became heavier. They approached the huge grey meccano arch of the Sydney Harbour Bridge, Carol's smooth, decisive driving and the hum of the car's air conditioner floating Sybil into a suspension of time. She would be content to sit silently by this beautiful woman and watch her hands on the wheel, the way she glanced up at the rear vision mirror, the angle of her chin, the firm lines of her mouth.

Carol turned her blonde head to meet Sybil's intent gaze. "We're almost there," she said to Sybil almost roughly, as if to break the moment.

* * * * *

Carol watched Sybil closely. She had identified the body as her husband and now was the time when shock could make her vulnerable, when she might say something unguarded, something incriminating. Sybil's face was so white the faint dusting of freckles across her cheeks and nose stood out clearly. Her eyes met Carol's. "Can we leave?" she said.

Carol drove efficiently through the busy inner city streets, seized a parking space with swift competence, and guided Sybil out of the car and into a little coffee shop. They sat in silence over their coffee cups, their knees almost touching at the small table.

Sybil could not raise her eyes. She watched Carol fiddle with a spoon and thought irrelevantly what long, sensitive fingers she had, staring fixedly at the black opal ring she wore — anything to avoid considering the thing she had just identified as her husband. A shudder of alarm shook her composure. She'd said it was Tony, but with the face so destroyed . . . what if she glanced over to the

71

door and saw him walking into the coffee shop, his features still intact?

"It was Tony, wasn't it?" she asked, looking up into Carol's eyes for reassurance. "I mean, it looked . . . I thought it was Tony, but now. . . ."

Carol thought of the murderers who cried when they saw their victims: who turned as white as Sybil when they viewed their handiwork. "You said you were sure," she said coldly.

Someone at another table laughed. Sybil stared blankly at Carol, who suddenly put a hand over hers and said, her voice warming as she spoke, "It's all right. Everything fits: his age, height, eye color. He was carrying a passport, driver's license, credit cards. Some English money as well as Australian." There was a pause. Carol removed her hand. "Have your coffee."

"I'm sorry. I can't drink it."

"Mrs. Quade? Shall we go?"

"Please. Call me Sybil." She glanced up with a bitter smile. "Looking at a dead body together rather dissolves formality, doesn't it?"

"You know my name is Carol. Come on, I'll drive you home."

"I should go back to school."

"Oh, I think you're excused for today."

* * * * *

Arriving punctually at eight on Friday morning, Mrs. Farrell was relieved to find the police had decided to vacate her office and move to the local police station. She was less pleased to find on her desk a note from Inspector Ashton requesting an appointment.

Mrs. Farrell had been chided by the Department for not keeping Sir Richard fully informed and she now found her desire to cooperate considerably weakened. She was heartily tired of Bill Pagett, his illustrious father, and now, to cap it all, the uproar the death of Sybil Quade's husband had caused. Last night the television news bulletins had blown the story of Tony Quade's death into a swelling gothic drama with alarming innuendos about the relationships between Mrs. Quade, her husband and Bill Pagett. Even worse, heavy hints had been dropped about Pagett's romantic activities with, as one breathless reporter exclaimed, "nubile young beach goddesses from Bellwhether High." Later that night her telephone had run hot: Sir Richard had called, the Director-General had called, the Minister for Education had called.

This afternoon she was to make the official statement she and the Departmental representative had labored over the day before. "After all, Phyllis, public education needs positive press," the Minister had said, "and it is not helped by the present situation. We've heard that muckraker, Pierre Brand, is going to do one of his in-depth exposés and I want you to get in first to scotch the rumor that anything untoward ever happened between Sir Richard's son and any senior girl."

Mrs. Farrell's suggestion that this statement might not be completely accurate was disregarded and she was now faced with the unhappy prospect of trying to please everyone at once — the Department, the Minister, Sir Richard, and the voracious media.

Her train of thought was interrupted by Lynne Simpson, who entered, uninvited, with a jangle of gold bracelets and an expression of deep concern. "Mrs. Farrell! I have been accosted, positively accosted, by a television crew in the car park. Surely you have the

73

authority to warn them off. I can't see how any teacher can be expected to cope with this type of harassment as well as the demands of a day's lessons. What are you going to do about it?"

"I'm rather surprised to see you here so early," said Mrs. Farrell, making a barbed reference to the number of mornings she had stood by the signing-in book as Lynne, late as usual, had swept in on a wave of breathless apology.

"First Bill and now Tony!" exclaimed Lynne, sitting uninvited on the nearest chair. "I feel it's a nightmare from which I'll never wake!"

Mrs. Farrell repressed a sarcastic reference to the fact that the two victims would certainly not awake this side of eternity, and dialed her deputy principal. Having dispatched him to clear the school grounds of cameras and reporters she turned her attention back to Lynne, who was checking her scarlet nail polish. "There is something else, Ms. Simpson?"

"Well, yes. I do need your advice."

Mrs. Farrell examined Lynne's expression of earnest entreaty, her smooth dark hair, the expensive rings and beautiful clothing. The only advice Lynne Simpson had ever asked of her before had related to manipulating the Department's leave formula to gain extra time off teaching duties during her divorce, so Mrs. Farrell waited with interest to see what special service she could render this time.

"It's about a threatening phone call. Last night. I just froze when I heard the whispering voice." Lynne's face wore a suitably alarmed expression as she continued, "I'm all alone. I've sent the kids to Bruce, of course, because I need to know they're safe, and away from all this. And as far as Bruce himself is concerned, I certainly don't want

74

him back, but it can be comforting at times to have a man around, don't you think?"

Mrs. Farrell thought of her own quiet little accountant husband: a comfort? Not quite the word. A presence, or even a habit, would be a better description. "Have you told the police?" she asked.

"Well, I expected to find them here, in your office. Where are they?"

Frostily amused at Lynne's aggrieved tone, Mrs. Farrell advised that the police had thought it more convenient to move to the local police station and continue their inquiries from that base. "However," she said, "Inspector Ashton will be here to see me at ten. If you wish, I'll advise her that you would like to see her."

Still Lynne did not rise. Mrs. Farrell sighed. "There's something more?"

"I wonder if you'll be speaking to the media, Mrs. Farrell."

"The Education Department has asked me to make a statement this afternoon. Why?"

Lynne leaned forward confidentially. "It's just," she said sincerely, "that sometimes it's better to give an exclusive, rather than be hounded by every little reporter with a notebook." Mrs. Farrell remained silent, so Lynne continued, "It happens that I have a contact with a television program, and I did say that I'd approach you to see if you'd be interested. . . ."

"In what way would I be interested?"

"Why, in giving an exclusive interview. You'd be paid, of course."

"By whom?"

Lynne radiated enthusiasm as she said, "*Behind the News* is the highest rated program in its time slot and

Pierre Brand must be one of the most skilled interviewers —"

Mrs. Farrell rose. "Definitely not. And please don't tout this offer round to other staff members. It could do nothing but harm for Bellwhether to be associated with the kind of sensationalism that Pierre Brand peddles every night of the week."

Lynne left Mrs. Farrell a whiff of her expensive perfume and a feeling of outrage. That a member of her staff should stoop to soliciting for Pierre Brand was almost as disgraceful as any expectation that she, Mrs. Farrell, would deign to be interviewed for a program she had always regarded as unreliable, exaggerated and of very poor taste.

Chapter Six

"Carol," said the Police Commissioner, "I want you to spend this weekend concentrating on the Quade woman. Yes, I know you're going to say you've got a lot of other work to clear up, but I'll deal with that. The point is, Sybil Quade could be the key to the whole thing. Obviously she's being less than frank about her relationships, both with her husband and with Sir Richard's son. I want you to win her trust, and fast, Carol — that bastard Pierre Brand is after the story and Sir Richard's getting restless, okay?"

* * * * *

When Carol had rung with the offer of a day puttering around the harbor in a little cabin cruiser, Sybil's immediate impulse had been to refuse, although she was tempted, not only by the chance to escape Terry's suffocating presence and the telephone calls from curious acquaintances, but also by the thought of spending more time with Carol.

"I have to ask you some further questions," said Carol, "and I rather selfishly hoped you'd agree to come out on the harbor, especially as I haven't had the time to use my boat for months. It would be an opportunity to combine some work with an amount of pleasure."

"It sounds great," Sybil heard herself saying.

* * * * *

So far there had been no questions. Carol had picked her up at seven and had driven her to her home. "My father built this house — he was an architect," said Carol as Sybil looked around. Clinging to the steep slope, the calm waters of Middle Harbour reflecting through the wide windows, the gum trees pressing in from every side, the house was private, beautiful and filled with light and an atmosphere of serenity. They hardly spoke.

Standing at the railing of the huge wooden deck looking out to water, sky, and bushland, Sybil felt herself relax, smile, stretch. "What a beautiful position," she said.

A kookaburra tried a preliminary chuckle, then launched into his full repertoire of raucous laughter. The air was still as wine; below them the water lay green in the early light, disturbed only by wind ripples and the oars of a rowing shell that looked rather like a beetle sculling on an elastic surface. Sybil turned back to the house, which rose in levels behind her up the hillside, its huge plate glass windows staring at the view. "You live alone?" she asked.

Alone? thought Carol. Do you want to fill my lonely bed? Aloud, she said: "I have a fat, lazy cat for company at night and the birds in the morning." She gestured at a gum tree whose top overhung the deck on which they stood. In patient rows sat several kookaburras and magpies. "They've become monsters," she said, putting chopped meat on the railing at one end and stepping back beside Sybil. "After nesting they bring their babies along for a free feed too, so I have a constantly rising population to supply. See the smaller magpies more grey-brown than black and white? They're the young ones. They travel in little packs and behave like delinquent children."

Watching the birds swoop to snatch the meat, Sybil said, "Do you ever get lonely?" She turned her head to find Carol's cool green eyes considering her.

"Sometimes," said Carol.

Sybil wanted to say: I feel lonely and I have no one to talk to, but she looked at Carol's still face and was silent.

Carol put a piece of meat on her palm and held it out. A large cream and brown kookaburra edged along the railing, leaned over and seized the morsel, giving it a quick whack on the railing before swallowing it. "Just in case it's still alive," said Carol, her face suddenly lit with a smile.

Sybil was astonished to feel a tug of desire. Confused, she looked away from Carol's mouth. "Can I try feeding one?" she heard herself say quite normally.

"The magpies are more daring — and greedy," said Carol, giving her several pieces of chopped meat.

79

Sybil concentrated on coaxing the big black and white birds to feed, stingingly aware of Carol standing behind her.

"All gone," said Carol to the birds, showing them the empty container. Sybil followed her inside, her eyes on the tanned legs beneath the white shorts. This is ridiculous, she told herself — it's just that I've been alone too long.

* * * * *

The small half-cabin launch glided over the smooth green water accompanied by the buzz of its outboard motor. They sat in silence, Sybil captivated by the little private bays, the small collections of seagulls apparently in deep contemplation, the gum trees with bulbous roots where the bushland came right down to the harbor, the warm tones of the weathered rocks. She glanced at Carol and was rewarded with a quick smile. Sybil smiled in return, swinging her gaze back to the moored boats through which the launch was threading its way. She found herself wanting to stare at Carol, to examine her, item by item, to locate the cause for the growing fascination she was feeling. She shook her head slightly. Perhaps it was the attraction of danger, the knowledge that the keen intelligence behind those startling eyes was assessing the possibility that she had killed two people.

"Do you mind where we go?" said Carol.

Sybil shook her head. For the first time in months she felt content. She knew she should keep up her guard, be careful, even suspicious, but an unexpected surge of delight filled her. "This is wonderful!" she exclaimed, laughing with pleasure. At once she felt a sense of guilt. Two days ago, on Thursday, she had identified Tony's

80

broken body. How could she lounge in this little boat relaxed and, for a moment, even happy?

Carol watched her expression change from laughter to cool control. "Have a go at steering," she said, wanting to see the delight on Sybil's face again.

"I don't think I'll be very good."

"There's plenty of room to weave all over the place, if you want to," said Carol, changing places. "I'll act like lightning if you head straight for the shore," she added with a grin.

They went deeper and deeper into the upper harbor, passing under Roseville Bridge and entering Davidson National Park. The waterway was now only a narrow stream, bush crowding both sides, and all signs of civilization had disappeared. Other launches glided by, their occupants in various stages of undress to catch the sun which was gaining strength as the morning advanced.

Taking back the controls, Carol selected a spot and brought the launch into the bank with smooth efficiency. "I don't suppose we can decently eat lunch until half past eleven at the earliest," she said, "but if you'd like a cup of coffee we can loll around for an hour or so and admire nature."

They spread out a rug in a little clearing near the water. Carol stripped to her bikini to bake her already brown body, and Sybil sat with her back against a tree, gazing out at the water and letting calmness seep into her mind. "Could you put some suntan cream on my back?" said Carol, sleepy in the sun.

Sybil took the plastic bottle almost reluctantly. Her fingers tingled as she spread the cream over Carol's smooth brown skin and she found herself wanting to fill the companionable silence with awkward conversation.

81

"Carol. . . ." she began as Carol turned her head to look up at her, speaking at the same time. They both laughed.

"Sorry," said Carol, "what were you saying?"

"Nothing important. I interrupted you," said Sybil, tensing with the realization that Carol must be about to spoil everything by asking the questions she had promised.

"It's just that I'm starving," said Carol, stretching and yawning. "I don't care what time it is, I insist we have lunch."

Carol had brought a hamper containing roast chicken, crusty bread and white wine. She's trying to soften me up, said Sybil to herself, aware that she welcomed the attempt, whatever the motive. Sprawled on the rug, surrounded by the hum of insects, the distant voices of people on the water, the shifting patterns of shade and sunlight, Sybil found herself letting go of much of her usual reserve. And as she relaxed more and more, the fact that Carol Ashton was a detective inspector of police faded to insignificance, and the events of the week receded like old headlines.

They spent the afternoon in lazy indolence, chatting, dozing, watching the bush birds in the branches overhead and the forays of countless insects drawn by the magnet of their picnic food. Then the air stirred with a stronger breeze and the sun became fainter.

"Southerly buster coming up," said Carol, "so we'd better make for home now, or risk a rough trip and a drenching."

Sybil looked back with affection as they cleared the bank and started to make headway back towards the main harbor. She couldn't remember a day she had enjoyed with such uncomplicated pleasure. She clambered to the front of the cabin and sat with her face turned to the wind and spray, laughing aloud as the waves, whipped by the rising wind, sent sheets of water over her.

Carol watched her from the tiller, amazed at the warmth and spontaneity one day had released. She smiled as Sybil turned and called above the buzz of the engine and the rising storm, gesturing at the lightning forking from the towering clouds that raced towards them from the south. Her red hair was wet with spray, her voice faint against the din. "Isn't this great!" she shouted.

The rain came down in torrents as they rounded a headland and started to beat down the harbor to Carol's mooring, so that they were soaked to the skin by the time they had scrambled, breathless, onto the jetty below the house. "Oh, Carol, thank you," said Sybil, "that was such fun."

Isn't it a pity, thought Carol, that I can't just enjoy your company. I have to start dissecting your relationships, asking you questions you don't want to answer. Now, when you're tired and relaxed and your guard is down, what will you tell me?

Carol didn't respond to Sybil's banter as they climbed the steps up to the house. She had deliberately picked Sybil up from her place, rather than let her drive herself, so she would have no ready escape route at the end of the day. Not that Sybil seemed to want escape. At Carol's suggestion she showered and changed into a pair of Carol's jeans and a T-shirt.

Now she sat sipping a brandy and contemplating her bare feet. "I think I've sunburned the very tops of my toes," she said with a laugh.

"Sybil, I do have to ask you some questions."

Carol watched the shutter come down over her face. "Yes?"

"I want you to discuss your relationship with your husband."

There was a long pause, then, squaring her shoulders, Sybil said, "Okay. What do you want to know?"

Sybil began to talk. Question and answer, slow consideration of a difficult or dangerous idea: but no laughter, no animation, no expression on her face or in her voice. Probing, encouraging, challenging, Carol led her to expand her answers until a three-dimensional picture began to build in Carol's mind.

Tony Quade had been good-looking, with a soft English voice and a shy silky charm. He could be witty, warm and considerate. He was also a consummate liar, a fact that Sybil had only realized after they were married. And in private he didn't bother to disguise the cruelty of his wit or the jealousy and possessiveness in his nature.

"Living with Tony was like being married to two different people. Often he was relaxed and pleasant, just as he appeared to people outside, but other times his mood changed, and he became the other Tony — the one I hated."

The kitchen was designed to be part of the living room, so while she scrambled eggs Carol continued to ask her questions, reluctant to let Sybil sink into silence and destroy the tenuous link of communication they had established between them. Sybil ate mechanically, her face blank. To Carol the change was extraordinary. The laughing, relaxed woman of the day had become the controlled, cool person she had first met.

"Why did you marry him?" she asked.

"I wish I knew. It seemed right at the time." She laughed ruefully. "I'd just about decided that no burning, passionate love affair was going to illuminate my life, so I was ready to settle for something more prosaic." She

84

played with her fork. "Tony seemed ideal, he filled a gap in my life, he said he loved me . . . all that sort of thing."

"Why did you separate?"

"I tried for too long to make it work. Do you understand? If I'd been honest with myself I'd have admitted it was a mistake from the beginning, but it was easier to stay with him than to face breaking up and all that would involve. In a way, I played a game, persuading myself that things were better than they were. And you know how our society thinks in couples. I suppose I thought it was more reasonable to be unhappy in a socially acceptable unit than to be alone and independent."

And what do you think now? thought Carol. What chances would you take for happiness? Aloud she said, "What changed your mind?"

Sybil shrugged. "It wasn't any one thing. It just became unbearable, so we separated."

"It was that easy?"

Sybil smiled bitterly. "Oh, it wasn't easy. Tony didn't want to accept it at all."

"Would you have gone ahead and divorced him, or was a legal separation enough?"

"I didn't want to marry anyone else."

"Not Bill Pagett?"

Sybil moved convulsively. "No!"

That got a reaction, Carol thought. She hated him, but why? "How about Terry Clarke? Have you thought of marrying him?"

The control was back. "No," she said calmly.

"Did your husband expect you to divorce him after the required year's separation?"

"No, he didn't. He hated to fail at anything. He was one of the most determined people I've ever met. I'm sure he was absolutely convinced I wouldn't go ahead and do it. He thought I'd come to my senses."

"Was he still in love with you?"

"Love?" said Sybil with a twist to her mouth. "I don't think so."

"Then why did he come back to Australia if it wasn't for a reconciliation with you?"

"I don't know why Tony came back. He didn't contact me."

"What about Bill Pagett? Did he say anything to you about him?"

Sybil sighed. "Bill didn't say anything," she said flatly. "I'm tired, Carol."

"I'll drive you home."

They didn't speak on the journey, each watching the tunnel of rain lit by the headlights and listening to the swish of the tires on the wet road. The street outside Sybil's house seemed to have been deserted by the media, who had taken to besieging her as she left or entered the school grounds. Carol caught her careful checking of parked cars and said, "I asked the local station to discourage them, but I'm afraid they'll be back." She turned up Sybil's steep drive. "I'll see you to the front door and then look around outside to make sure everything's all right."

Sybil was suddenly aware that she must have a gun with her, and the sense of danger, absent all day, rushed back to surround her.

The stone steps were slippery from the warm rain and it was so dark that Sybil had difficulty seeing her way. "Be careful," she said over her shoulder. She was acutely aware of Carol directly behind her on the steps, so when she slipped it was not surprising to find Carol's arm supporting her. What astonished Sybil was her own reaction. She found herself turning within the half embrace, until their lips met so naturally that Sybil had melted into the kiss before she realized exactly what was happening. Then it was too late to stop, too late to think, too late to be sensible. In the darkness they kissed urgently, passionately, Carol's arms tight around her.

Alarm began to ring insistently in Sybil's mind. Burning, she thrust Carol away, broke the circle of her arms, and fled up the wet steps to the front door. Carol didn't follow. Sybil fumbled with the key and finally wrenched the door open. She turned on the outside light to dispel the dangerous darkness. Jeffrey darted up the steps, wound around Sybil's legs and then walked delicately inside. From below Carol's clear voice said, "Sybil? Are you all right?"

She laughed without humor. "I'm great!" she said, and went into the house, shutting the door firmly behind her.

* * * * *

Carol was very conscious that Mark Bourke was occupying the same chair where Sybil had laughingly contemplated her sunburned toes the evening before. In contrast, there was nothing light-hearted about Mark this Sunday morning. He was grimly plowing through the report that had kept him up half the night. He smothered a yawn and handed Carol neatly typed pages.

"That's all the people who could conceivably have some motive to kill either Bill Pagett or Tony Quade," he said, "and you'll see it's wide open as far as opportunity is concerned. There's hardly a decent alibi for anyone, which isn't unusual." As Carol frowned over the pages he added, "And I have got one interesting bit of information about

87

Tony Quade from England. It seems his uncle was a forensic pathologist of some note, so he certainly had plenty of opportunity to find out how to kill someone with a power drill. Pity Tony's dead himself, otherwise he'd be the perfect suspect."

"He could have been Pagett's murderer, and then either suicided or been murdered himself, although I think it's highly unlikely," said Carol.

"I think it comes back to Sybil Quade. No doubt during their marriage they had many little heart-to-hearts where he had the opportunity to drop this little lethal tidbit about power drill murder."

"I don't suppose you thought to ask about similar cases in Britain?"

Bourke looked suitably hurt. "Of course I did. And, fascinatingly enough, Tony Quade's uncle gave evidence in a celebrated case where it was an iron spike driven into the base of the skull of the victim. All that's happened here is progress — the murder's been mechanized, so to speak."

Carol frowned. "I don't see how we can find out if Quade knew about this iron spike murder from his uncle, let alone if he discussed it at a dinner party, or whatever."

"I'll ask around," said Bourke, "but you're right, it's going to be pretty impossible."

Carol went back to the report, reading through the pages with disciplined concentration. "Mark, this statement of Hilary Cosgrove's — it doesn't tell us anything."

Mark looked grim. "It wasn't very pleasant trying to get it. Poor kid, she'd cried herself into exhaustion, and her parents hovered around to protect her. I'm sure she knows something, but I'm damned if I could get it out of her."

"Let's give her a day or so, then try again," said Carol. "How did the interview with Lynne Simpson go? More successful?"

"It was kind of you to pass her on to me," said Bourke with a grin. "She tells me she likes to have a man around at all times."

"You a candidate?" asked Carol, amused.

Bourke feigned surprise. "You know we can't get emotionally involved with anyone on a case," he said with mock severity. "I'm surprised you even mentioned it. Besides, I'd much rather latch on to Sybil Quade. I'm a pushover for cool women with red hair. I just know there's a fire burning down there, somewhere."

"Can we get back to Lynne Simpson?" Carol asked abruptly.

Bourke flipped through his notebook. "Here we are: Lynne Simpson started off by saying how surprised she was that I was interviewing her, and not you. Didn't the Inspector want to speak to her personally about such important evidence? I said you were very busy. That didn't impress her at all, but my boyish charm finally wore her down and she launched into a full description of the threatening phone call . . . that's when she said she always liked to have a man around the place."

Carol didn't feel like light conversation. "The call?" she prompted.

Mark's grin faded. "As far as she can remember, this is it: a throaty, whispering voice said, 'Lynne, darling, I've got a little hatchet just for you. One good whack will split open your head and spill out all your brains. Send you up to heaven, Lynne darling.' Then the caller disconnected."

"Called back?"

"Of course. A few minutes later. This one repeated the first sentence and then, just for variety, said, 'Chop off all your fingers and toes. Be sure to wear nail polish that goes with blood.' "

Carol wrinkled her nose. "Revolting little touch," she said. "Did she seem frightened?"

Mark spread his hands. "Peeved, more than anything — and maybe a bit uneasy. Certainly not terrified."

"Does she suspect anyone?"

Mark grinned. "Funny you should say that. You remember Edwina Carter said she would be delighted if she could accuse Lynne Simpson of making the threatening call to her? Well, our Lynne blames Edwina. She says Edwina has a bitter, twisted soul, and it's obvious that Edwina would get a charge out of frightening her. She did concede she had no evidence, but she does have what she described as 'a deep, deep conviction.' " He looked up. "Oh, and one interesting thing — Lynne said she knew Edwina had claimed to get an anonymous phone call, but it was obvious to Lynne that she was just saying that to protect herself."

"I can't believe it's a coincidence that falling off a cliff is mentioned in Edwina Carter's call, and then Tony Quade obligingly tumbles off the headland," said Carol.

"No, which means it was made by the murderer, or someone who knew what was going to happen, and, working to Lynn's theory, that person is Edwina herself."

"Could be anyone," said Carol, rubbing her eyes.

"You look as tired as I feel," said Bourke.

"I didn't sleep very well," said Carol, with the wry thought that she had made the understatement of the year. "Come on, Mark, let's go through the rest of this. I've got an appointment with Sir Richard at two o'clock, and he's expecting a full report."

"With the murderer signed, sealed and delivered?"

"Hardly, but somewhere he or she's slipped up."

90

"I don't know," said Bourke, "this one's awfully sharp, and laughing at us, I think.

*****

Sir Richard's home was rather more ostentatious than the palatial residences around it. Carol negotiated the gently curving drive to stop in front of a house that was a monument to money and bad taste. It wanted nothing: wide stone steps led to a massive entrance door flanked by two huge stone lions, the building squatting like a fat white cake behind them. She glanced at the sweeping lawns and ornate fountain as she rang the doorbell, imagining how she would landscape the grounds with native trees to attract the birds.

Sir Richard opened the door himself. He looked tired, but as impressive as ever. They exchanged pleasantries as he led her to his sumptuous study. One wall was lined with books, and the predictable large leather-topped desk dominated the room. Incongruously, it seemed to Carol, a huge stuffed blue marlin hung over the open fireplace. Sir Richard followed her eyes and smiled complacently. "Caught it myself off the Queensland coast a year or so ago," he said. "Near record. Hope to do better next time."

Sir Richard rang for coffee, and then turned his formidable attention on Carol. She had met him often, but not usually alone. He had about him an aura of power which had not been even slightly diminished by his retirement from politics, so she was not surprised that he knew every development in the case. He had only to ask, and he would receive whatever he wanted.

"That girl, the one Bill was supposed to be involved with, have you interviewed her?"

"Hilary Cosgrove. Detective Sergeant Bourke saw her on Friday. She was too upset before then."

"I'm not surprised. She's pregnant," said Sir Richard.

Carol's expression didn't change. "I didn't know that. Your son?"

"So she claimed. He told me about it last Saturday night. I advised him to persuade her to get rid of it. It would hardly do Bill any good to be associated with a scandal over a schoolgirl, would it?"

"And?"

"And nothing. He wasn't keen on the idea, but he agreed to talk to her about it the next day."

"Do you know if he did?"

"I rang him on Sunday afternoon. He said he was seeing her that evening, and that he'd be in touch later. That was the last time I spoke to him." He carefully unwrapped a cigar. "You smoke? No? You don't mind if I do?" He leaned back in his leather chair. "This kid, Hilary Cosgrove, could she have killed him?"

"It's not impossible. She wasn't at school on Monday. She stayed home, alone, saying she had a stomach upset. She could have walked down to the school, but if she did, no one saw her."

Sir Richard grunted, and changed the subject. "How are your investigations going with Peter McIvor?"

"We know he owed your son five thousand dollars, and he was having trouble paying it back."

"Ah, yes, the gambling club." Sir Richard smiled faintly. "You know, of course, that my son was keen on gambling, and the Pink Dolphin Club, the one he introduced McIvor to, is illegal."

Carol nodded. It was strongly rumored that Sir Richard's money had set up the Pink Dolphin Club and other successful illegal gambling casinos. "A teacher's salary doesn't seem to be enough to meet your son's expenses," she said mildly.

"Oh, it wasn't. I paid him an allowance. But he loved teaching, Inspector, he really did. Frankly, I wanted him in business, but he had neither the brains nor the inclination. He liked swimming, sailing, doing things with his hands . . . so he became an industrial arts teacher on the Peninsula. For him, it was an ideal life."

With access to an endless supply of young girls who were too young to threaten his masculinity, thought Carol. Aloud she said, "Do you have any information that could help the investigation?"

"I have confidence in your abilities, Inspector. You know, of course, about Alan Witcombe's activities?"

"Yes."

Sir Richard blew smoke reflectively towards the ceiling. "And then there's Sybil Quade," he said.

Carol's pulse leaped at her name. "The Commissioner feels Mrs. Quade is a central figure," she said neutrally.

"So do I," said Sir Richard. "Bill often mentioned her, especially after her marriage to Quade broke up."

"In what way?"

Sir Richard smiled. "She's a very attractive woman, isn't she? Bill found her so, anyway. I don't think they were just friends, if you see what I mean."

"Mrs. Quade denies any intimacy."

"I'm sure she does. Wouldn't you, in her place? Besides, I believe she has someone else interested in her — Terry Clarke. He strikes me as the jealous sort. Are you following that up?"

"We're following everything up," said Carol.

"Good," said Sir Richard, standing. The meeting was obviously at an end. "I do appreciate you coming here personally, Inspector, and I expect that you will be making considerable progress in this coming week."

"I trust so," said Carol, unable to keep the irritation out of her voice.

This seemed to amuse Sir Richard, who left her with a smile and the words, "I have absolute confidence in you, Inspector, otherwise you wouldn't be on the case."

Bastard, thought Carol as she drove away.

Chapter Seven

The dawn sky was an unpleasant, curdled red. Gray clouds hung oppressively low and a stiff hot breeze blew against Sybil's face as she sat on the beach, her arms around her legs and her chin resting on her knees. Suddenly she became conscious that someone had approached to stand behind her. Her heart caught as she realized it was Carol. "How did you know where to find me?"

Carol had been running. Her T-shirt was wet and her breath short. "Don't you remember? Mark Bourke took exhaustive details of everyone's morning schedules. You said you usually went for an early swim. I run every morning, so I decided to drive down to the beach and jog along the sand, taking the chance you'd be here." She sank down beside her. "We need to discuss what happened on Saturday night."

"Nothing happened."

"Okay. Good. That's it." Carol stood up. "Sorry to interrupt you."

"Carol, stop. Please, sit down again." She watched Carol sit, unlace her running shoes and wriggle her toes in the sand.

There was a long pause. Seagulls squabbled, the water ran up the beach in scallops towards their feet, a passing dog stopped to check them out before going busily on his way. Sybil, keeping her eyes resolutely turned towards the waves, was aware of how often Carol let silence drag on until someone had to break it. It's a technique, she thought, knowing that she would be driven to speak first. For the first time for as long as she could remember, she gave herself the luxury of dropping her guard and saying exactly what she really felt. "I want you to know that Saturday, on the harbor — somehow I felt I was living more vividly than I have for years. It was as thougt everything, what I saw, what I felt, was more real and more significant than ever before." She turned to meet Carol's green eyes. "And that kiss was wrong, but it was so exciting."

Carol looked away.

"Are you going to say anything?" asked Sybil.

What can I say to you, thought Carol, when you think to kiss is wrong? She forced a casual tone as she said, "Sybil, it was no big deal. Let's forget it — it won't happen again."

96

Sybil's voice was rough with resentful anger. "That's the trouble Carol, I want it to happen again."

Of course you do, straight woman, Carol thought bitterly. Forbidden fruit is so exciting, isn't it? And you'll fuck up my life, say you're sorry, and walk back to your safe world.

She stood up abruptly, brushing the sand from her shorts. Sybil joined her and they began to pace along the wet sand above the water line. Carol's silver voice was tight. "I'm a police officer. I'm investigating a murder, possibly two. You were involved with both of the victims. There is no way that we can have any relationship, and that includes being friends."

Sybil asked the question that had bounced in her head since Saturday night: "Have you ever made love to a woman?"

"Yes," said Carol flatly. They stopped to face each other. "Have you?"

Sybil turned away and began to walk up through the soft, dry sand to her towel. She snatched it up and flicked it savagely to get rid of clinging particles. "No. It's unnatural. It's wrong."

Carol let out her breath in a long sigh. "Well, you have no problem, then. Just forget it."

Sybil stared at her, then turned and strode off towards the car park. Over her shoulder she said, "Why did you come here this morning?"

They came to a halt beside Sybil's car. Carol jangled her car keys. "I've no idea," she said with a shrug.

Sybil watched her as she walked away, but she didn't look back.

* * * * *

"Been trying to get you," said Bourke as Carol walked into Bellwhether police station.

"I was out running. What's up?"

Bourke gestured to the desk. "Possible weapon. Looks like blood and some hair on it. Thought you'd like to see it before it went to Science."

Carol considered the varnished wooden surface. "Baseball or softball bat."

"Yes, and government issue. Look at the lettering stamped on the haft. I'll bet it comes from Bellwhether High School's sports supplies. Kid found it on the headland near where Quade fell. Don't know how we missed it when we searched, but it was on a narrow ledge a couple of meters from the top."

"Thrown down there or deliberately hidden?"

"Don't know. The kid found it, picked it up, was sharp enough to think it might be important, but he took it home with him before he rang us. He's in the other room. Do you want to see him?"

"No. Take him back to the headland after you fingerprint him, Mark. And take a photographer and a couple of officers with you. I want the place searched again in case we've missed something else."

She sat down at the desk Bourke had been using and checked through the papers until she found a full timetable for the school. Wednesday afternoon was reserved for sport. She leafed through the pages to the supervision schedule. There it was, blankly staring at her: Senior Baseball. Bellwhether Oval. Supervisors: S. Quade and P. McIvor. She had a vivid picture of Sybil clutching a baseball bat — swinging it in a looping arc — the dull whack as it connected with her husband's skull.

She pushed the image out of her mind and concentrated on the other name. Pete McIvor? She visualized his open, immature face. He was the sort who would blush with guilt if he evaded a bus fare. She ran the interview with him through her mind. He had constantly smoothed his mustache, shifting in his seat and clearing his throat at every question, however innocuous. But that could be a very sound way to behave if you were hiding something. A high level of anxiety for harmless queries could be used to mask genuine alarm when dangerous questions were asked.

During the time Pagett had been murdered Pete had no corroboration of his movements until he began teaching in the first period of the day. He claimed to have gone to assembly and then to the book room to collect textbooks for distribution to his first class. He was always very punctual, and that Monday morning had been no exception. Bourke had checked that he had distributed the textbooks at the beginning of the lesson, though of course he could have collected them from the book room at any time.

The coroner had given Tony Quade's probable time of death as somewhere between ten and twelve o'clock on Wednesday night, the warm night and the complication of cooler sea breezes making it difficult to be more accurate. Bourke had confirmed that Pete McIvor had been at the pub with friends until about eleven, when he had announced he was going home. Although he shared a flat with two other people, one had been out when he had arrived and the other was very vague about the time, so Pete certainly had the opportunity to dispose of Tony Quade if he had wanted to.

She turned to the notes on Sybil. At the very beginning of the assembly she had taken the microphone to give details of an excursion to the drama theatre of the Opera House. She said she then went down to stand by the students, but no one remembered her definitely being there. Then, because she didn't have a roll call or a first lesson, she was free to go to Bill Pagett's workroom and kill him. She said she was sitting in her empty classroom preparing lessons, but no one had seen her there.

As far as her husband was concerned, the day before he died Carol had confronted Sybil with the note she had written to Pagett and the results of the tests on the power drill in her garage. Carol had left her silent and white-faced. Had she then coolly planned to meet her husband so that she could kill him before he was able to incriminate her in some way?

Carol stared at the papers in her hands. Be objective, she thought — wanting her not to be guilty doesn't make her so.

* * * * *

Terry was furious. Ignoring the others in the staff room, he confronted Sybil. "Where'd you go Saturday? Why wouldn't you see me yesterday? Syb? I want an answer."

"Will you shut up! I'm trying to mark essays," snapped Lynne.

Alan Witcombe thought it politic to intervene: "Yes, Terry, we're all very upset, but please do show some consideration. It's a difficult time —"

"Mind your own business!"

Before Alan could respond to this challenge to his position, there was a knock at the staff room door.

Terry snatched it open. "Well, what do you want?"

The small student, intimidated, said with a rush, "Ms. Simpson's lunch. Asked me to get it for her. From the tuckshop."

Terry took it from him, and he scuttled away. "Think everyone's your servant?" he said, dumping the lunch on Lynne's pile of essays.

"It gives the kids a sense of responsibility," said Lynne airily. "Besides, they love running messages."

Terry grunted, and turned back to Sybil. "I want to know what you did this last weekend."

Sybil felt she could scream with frustrated irritation. "Please Terry, I'll speak to you later," she said in an effort to placate him.

"When? When later? I want a time."

"After school. I'll ring you."

"All right," said Terry, "I'll follow you home, straight after the final bell."

Sybil felt trapped and angry, but before she could speak Edwina, blinkworthy in luminescent green, said, "Terry, I'm so sorry to upset your plans, but Syb's promised to call in to my place for a cup of coffee after school." She beamed at his frown. "We girls must stick together at times like this, you know," she said archly, "and who knows how long Syb will be? It would be much better if she rang you when she got home, wouldn't it?"

Hiding her surprise at this unexpected invitation, Sybil said briskly, "Yes, Terry. I'll ring you, okay?"

Terry nodded and stalked out of the staff room. "Dear, dear," said Edwina. "He's so possessive, isn't he? Dangerously possessive, do you think, Syb?"

She smiled at Sybil's resigned expression. "You sure can pick them," she said. "Come to my place straight after school, I think you need to escape for a while."

* * * * *

101

Sybil drove to Edwina's house with her teeth clenched so tightly her jaw ached. She felt battered by demands and emotions, filled at one moment with bitter anger, and the next with helpless anxiety.

Detective Bourke had contacted her to make an appointment at lunchtime. She expected Carol to be with him, and was disconcerted to find him alone in the deputy's office. Unable to resist, she heard herself saying, "Is Inspector Ashton here?" and was startled at the shaft of disappointment when he shook his head.

She answered his questions about the supply and storage of sports equipment with a puzzled frown. "Surely Physical Education could help you more than I could," she said.

He smiled and continued. She wanted to know why he was so interested in the bats, although, suddenly, she knew the answer. "Was one used. . . ." she began. Bourke looked encouraging. Sybil retreated. "I'm sorry," she said, "I didn't mean to interrupt you." A few more questions, then Bourke had thanked her and she left to walk back to the staff room. She had walked unheeding through the lunchtime din, thinking of Carol.

As Sybil parked outside Edwina's fence she was surprised to see Lynne's RX7 draw up behind her. Lynne slid languidly out of the seat and waited for Sybil to lock her car.

Edwina met them at the open front door, full of enthusiasm. "Hi. Come on in. Slipped out a few minutes early to beat you home. Have you two noticed how Farrell's losing her grip? She isn't patrolling the school perimeters with her usual regularity, is she?"

Lynne was amused. "Lucky she isn't. I've cut enough classes short in the last few days to earn an official reprimand." She glanced at Sybil. "We aren't all

102

conscientious saints like you, Syb. Besides, the way I feel at the moment, facing a difficult class is enough to send me off into screaming hysterics."

Edwina raised her eyebrows. "Frankly, Lynne, dear, I can't see you having anything but simulated hysterics at any time. Those of us privileged to know you well realize beneath that glossy exterior there beats a similarly glossy, hard heart."

Lynne just laughed at Edwina's sarcastic words. Sybil looked from one to the other. In what uneasy alliance did they stand? Their usual relationship ranged from indifference to loathing. "Did you ask me here for some particular reason?" she asked Edwina.

Edwina ignored the question, leading them to the back veranda overlooking the sheltered waters of Pittwater. Sybil's eyes followed the yachts tacking against the breeze. But however serene the view, she couldn't relax. "Edwina?" she prompted.

"The fact is," said Edwina, smugly confidential, "both Lynne and I have been approached by Pierre Brand for exclusive interviews."

Sybil said nothing. I'm learning the value of silence from Carol, she thought fleetingly.

"Pierre really is the most delightful man," said Lynne, to fill an awkward pause. She smiled at Sybil. "Anyway, Syb, he asked us if we could arrange for him to meet you, especially as you don't seem keen to speak to reporters."

"Not seem keen! Lynne, I won't speak to anyone. I don't want to discuss anything. I don't want to be photographed, pawed over, chewed up and spat out by Pierre Brand or anyone else."

The doorbell rang. Edwina bounced up to answer it, returning a moment later with Pierre Brand in tow.

103

Sybil stood to go.

"Oh, not yet, Syb," exclaimed Edwina, "Pierre's just arrived."

Brand thrust out his hand. "Mrs. Quade, please accept my condolences. I know this must be a very difficult time for you."

Sybil shook his hand reluctantly. He was smaller than he appeared on television, but he had the same slightly plastic, artificial air. Sybil imagined ripping open his shirt and finding circuits and switches. "I was just leaving," she said.

"There's a great deal of public interest in this case," said Pierre Brand smoothly, "particularly because of Sir Richard's son. A painless interview, a few moments of your time — that's all I ask."

"No."

He smiled ingratiatingly. "And it's to your advantage. As soon as the other media people know that you've signed an exclusive contract with my program, they'll leave you alone."

"No interview."

"Has Edwina mentioned a payment? My channel can afford to be generous when such an important story breaks."

Sybil shook her head. "You're very persistent, Mr. Brand, but the answer is still no. Now, I'm sorry, I have to go."

"Please, take my card. Ring me day or night when you change your mind, or even if you'd just like to discuss things with me. I think you'll find, upon reflection, that I'm offering a valuable opportunity."

How like Terry he is, thought Sybil, wanting something from me and not really caring how he gets it or what it means. "Please don't waste your card," she said, handing it back to him.

Edwina followed her out to the car. "Syb, no offense. Didn't think you'd take it this way."

"How do you think I'd take it!"

A sulky resentment rose in Edwina's face as Sybil let her anger show, and glancing back as she rounded the corner Sybil could see her standing slack-armed, her head turned to watch her go.

* * * * *

At home she was restless, fretful and impatient with herself. She glared at the recording equipment. All it did was invade her privacy. There had been no further threatening calls, and she didn't expect any more. Whoever it was had other plans. She dialed Terry's number and was irrationally annoyed when he snatched it up on the second ring.

She lied without compunction. "Look, Terry, I've got a splitting headache. I've taken something and I'm going to bed. For God's sake, I know it's only six o'clock. There's some law that says I can't go to bed this early? Don't badger me! All right, tomorrow night. Yes, we'll have dinner. Okay. Sorry about tonight. Bye."

She paced around, getting a drink, nibbling corn chips, cuddling the cat. Sybil knew she was in that unsettled state where she could neither sit still nor move with any purpose. Finally she turned on the television and flung herself into a chair. Her wandering attention was suddenly riveted by the sight of herself in the school car park.

"Sybil Quade, close friend of Sir Richard's murdered son, was too upset to be interviewed about the new and even more dreadful tragedy in her life," the voice-over said enthusiastically, "as mystery surrounds the death of her estranged husband, Tony Quade, who was found broken and bruised at the bottom of Bellwhether Headland by a young student of Bellwhether High." The picture switched to a long shot of the school with several kids clowning for the camera. "This is where," the voice continued cheerfully, "Sir Richard's son met his death in the bizarre Black and Decker murder, as yet unsolved."

Sybil's heart turned as the picture switched to a close-up of Carol, the voice continuing with a few flattering comments on her career. Then followed a brief interview, with Carol, confident and patient, answering reporters' questions.

As the next story began, Sybil found a card in her purse and sat biting her lip. She switched off the television and stood uncertainly by the phone. She stared at the recording equipment attached to it, then flipped open the lid and removed the tape. She unwillingly dialed the number, saying as soon as the receiver was picked up, "Carol?"

After the slightest pause, the calm silver voice replied, "Yes?"

Sybil shut her eyes, imagining Carol's face. "I want to see you."

"Has something happened?"

"No."

"Sybil, I don't. . . ."

"Please."

A pause, then: "I'll be there in about an hour. Is that okay?"

As she put down the receiver, Sybil released her breath in a long sigh. She replaced the tape cassette in the recorder, then moved restlessly around the house, unable

106

to concentrate, even to sit down. Why had she rung Carol against her will and certainly against her better judgment? Why was she pacing like a nervous kid waiting for a date?

Carol was ten minutes early and unnervingly polite. Sybil felt a jolt seeing the reality after the image on the television screen. "Would you like a drink?"

Carol shook her head. "Why did you call me?" she said.

Sybil was swept with a totally unexpected rage. "I couldn't help it! I didn't want to or mean to!" In the silence that followed her anger evaporated. "Carol, you feel it too, don't you?"

Carol smiled ruefully and turned away to gaze out at the sea. "Yes."

The insistent tingle of desire began to spread a slow fire in Sybil. "It's just some kind of physical thing, Carol. It'll go, I know it will."

Carol turned, saying mockingly, "A couple of cold showers and we'll be all right?" She saw Sybil's expression and her smile faded.

The air vibrated between them as their eyes locked. "Oh, God," said Sybil, "I feel as if I'm addicted to you." Her eyes dropped to Carol's mouth. "You're not going to ask me to go cold turkey are you?"

Carol was breathing as though she had been running. "Sybil, we have to be sensible."

"Can we be sensible tomorrow?"

Carol's mouth was as deliciously responsive as she remembered it, her arms as strong. Sybil struggled to stand back from herself, to see her want as an irrational physical need, but she began to drown in Carol's presence, in the warmth of her skin and the rhythm of her heartbeat. She could not remember feeling like this before

107

— safe and afraid at the same time, torn between the rightness of her actions and the conviction that they were wrong.

Carol began to undress her slowly, letting her hands slide across Sybil's ribs, around her back, down her hips, all the time kissing her with a controlled passion that aroused Sybil until she was seized with such impatient desire she gasped against Carol's mouth, "Not too long."

Carol lowered her gently onto the couch and, kneeling beside it, began to run her fingertips over Sybil's naked body in complex patterns, weaving paths of sensation that sang in corresponding paths of light against her closed eyelids. She arched under the soft brush of her hands. "Carol, please. I can't stand it."

"You can."

And now Carol's fingers were in her, and she pushed herself up against their pressure. She was floating in the most exquisite pain, knowing that it would soon explode in waves of release. But the tension grew higher and higher, the sensation more unbearably delightful, until she heard herself call out. And then she came in great shuddering waves that went on and on until she sank exhausted and smiling.

She opened her eyes. Carol, still fully dressed, sat on the floor, her face hidden against Sybil's side, her pale hair tickling Sybil's bare skin. "Carol, look at me."

Carol turned her head. "This must never happen again," she said.

Sybil sat up, her hands on Carol's shoulders. "Do you believe I killed Bill? And Tony? Do you really believe I could do that?" She watched the indecision on Carol's face. "Tell me what you really think — not a lie."

"I want to believe you had nothing to do with either."

"You want to believe, but you don't know, do you? Is that it?"

"Sybil. . . ."

"You'd arrest me if you thought me guilty, would you?"

Carol shook herself free and stood up. "Of course. I'd have to."

Sybil was shaken with anger and fear. Her voice rose as she said, "You make love to me, even though you think I'm capable of murder? Aren't you frightened of me? Don't you worry I might slip a knife between your ribs?"

Carol's face had grown hard with a matching anger, but her voice remained even. "I didn't realize you had a motive to kill me."

She wanted to slap Carol, shake her, hurt her in some way. Where Carol had been slow and careful undressing her, Sybil was rough. She felt the pulse pounding in Carol's throat and knew with a twisting exultation Carol wanted her so much that she could be defeated, as if she were an enemy.

Sybil pushed her back into a deep chair, kneeling between her outstretched legs. Carol's eyes were closed, her head thrown back, the light catching the line of her jaw. Sybil, aroused, angry and determined to dominate, slid her mouth across the hollows of Carol's throat. The nipples under her fingers were hard, the tanned skin sweet. She sank her teeth into Carol's shoulder much harder than she intended and was excited by the murmur of protest. I'll control you, I'll play you, I'll make your body sing for me, she thought.

The world became Carol's body. She slid her fingers into the wetness and Carol closed around them tighter and tighter.

The scent of Carol's body was at once familiar and strange. How could I ever imagine doing this, Sybil thought, her mouth seeking and finding the center of sensations. Carol's breath caught in her throat. Her hands were in Sybil's hair. "Ah, darling," she gasped.

The word spun in Sybil's head. Darling? Carol had only said that in an excess of passion, not as a term of love. Not that Sybil wanted love, she wanted nothing, especially not this physical obsession, not this consuming need. Carol had grown still, rigid — and then, sucking against Sybil's fingers, her climax began. Sybil raised her head and watched the convulsions ripple through Carol's body and then the calmness descend, knowing bleakly she was as near to love as she dared to be.

* * * * *

Sybil slept late and woke tired and heavy. Although she knew she should hurry or she would be late for school, she lay there while the events of the evening rushed back: how Carol had calmly dressed, not meeting her eyes; how stilted their conversation had been — and Carol's last words, "We just have to forget this."

Sybil had smiled at that. "I'll try," she had said.

And when Carol had gone, she remembered the mixture of guilt, alarm and excitement that had filled her. Lying here, images of making love danced behind her closed eyelids and she groaned, half in pleasure, half in exasperation as she began to burn with reawakened desire. How long before she got over this obsession with another woman? How long before this unnatural passion burnt itself out?

Driving to school, she tried to be honest with herself. She wanted to make love to Carol again, and again, and again. It was obviously a mindless physical need to be satisfied before she could resume a normal life. It wasn't love, and never could be — rather, it was an infatuation that had been caused by the circumstances and her own loneliness. And what was last night to Carol? An unwelcome interlude because it threatened her career? It wouldn't have the shattering impact it had had on Sybil. After all, Carol had said she'd made love to another woman, or was it women? Sybil felt an unexpected stab of jealousy. Was Carol in a relationship now? Did someone else taste that mouth and feel those fingers?

She swerved to avoid a cyclist who wobbled out from the curb, suddenly aware of how little attention she was paying to driving. With an effort of will she tried to push Carol out of her thoughts, but the moment she relaxed her concentration the pictures seeped back — images of bare skin, of her mouth, eyes, hair — the sound of her silver voice — and with them a longing for her so frightening in its intensity that she caught her breath. "This is just great, Sybil," she said with an angry irony.

* * * * *

Bourke put his head round the door. "The Lab rang to say the baseball bat matches Pagett's head wound, so it could've been used in both murders. The blood and hair are from Quade, though. And Alan Witcombe wants to see you. He says it's urgent." Carol nodded. Bourke continued, "I'm off to see Hilary Cosgrove again. Her father rang and said she was well enough to answer some more questions this morning. He also confirmed what Sir Richard told you. She is pregnant."

111

"Could her boyfriend, what's his name — Evan Berry? Could he have known about the baby? It'd give him even more of a motive," said Carol.

"I'll see what I can find out."

* * * * *

Alan Witcombe folded his angular body into a chair and glared at Carol. "I'll not have my wife subjected to filth!"

"I'm sorry?"

"Because my wife's a light sleeper, she answered the phone when it rang about three this morning. She was horrified to hear a stream of obscenities!"

"What was said?"

"I would not ask Alice to repeat what she heard. Sufficient to say that she hung up as quickly as possible. She woke me, and then the phone rang again."

"And you answered it this time."

"Of course. It was some sick, depraved person, spewing forth disgusting allegations in a hoarse whisper."

"Did you recognize the voice?"

"No, but I don't think it was a student. What are you going to do about it?"

"We can have Telecom intercept all incoming calls to your number and vet them before your phone rings."

Witcombe was waspish. "Apart from that perfectly obvious step, what are you doing about finding this pervert? It's probably the same person who killed Pagett."

"There may be some link. Could you write down what was said to you as accurately as possible, please. I'm sure

112

you know you're not the only person to receive these calls."

Witcombe was reluctant to record the words in writing, but Carol finally persuaded him to cooperate. Handing over the sheet he said, "It's the moral climate in the school, you know, Inspector. Corruption breeds violence."

Carol was interested in details about the corruption, but apart from an accurate assessment of Bill Pagett's character and activities, he was very vague about details and strong on broad, general impressions. Carol read through the words he had handed her. "The person actually started with 'Alan, Alan darling?' " she said, "Didn't this make you think it might be a woman?"

"Why? The degenerate who made this call wouldn't worry about details like that. Have you read it all? Sick!"

The call had contained a series of libelous comments about Witcombe's sexual inclinations and activities with both males and females, none mentioned by name, until the last — 'Syb's a randy little bitch for you, isn't she? Do anything to get it. Have you rammed it home, yet, Alan darling?'

Even Carol's vivid imagination couldn't imagine Alan Witcombe and Sybil in each other's arms. Disconcertingly, she had a sudden vision of Sybil and Terry making love. She forced herself to listen to Witcombe as he said, "Pagett deserved to die for what he did, but no one had the right to kill him." A look of satisfaction crossed his face. "But at least he's facing judgment now, and he can do no more damage."

* * * * *

113

Bourke came back bubbling with news. "Wait till you hear. It's the redhead we most admire, our Sybil."

Carol tensed. "Yes?" she said.

"When I told Hilary Cosgrove we knew she planned to see Pagett on Sunday night, she denied it at first, but after a while I broke her down. She admitted sneaking out and walking up the hill from her place — it takes about ten minutes. She says she'd just entered Pagett's driveway when she heard a loud argument and then a series of crashes and angry voices. She wasn't sure what to do, and while she was standing there, Sybil Quade comes flying out of the house, leaps into her car, and roars off so fast she nearly skittles Hilary."

"She's sure it was Sybil Quade?"

"Positive. Hilary's in her English class."

"Did she hear any of the argument clearly?"

"No, only 'you bastard' from Sybil. And she says she thinks she was crying when she ran out of the house."

"What happened then?"

"She said she was confused. She started to walk home again, got halfway down the hill, and then changed her mind. She went back, knocked on the door, and Pagett let her in."

"And?"

Bourke looked pleased. "The really interesting bit is this," he said. "When Hilary went into Pagett's place, she found he wasn't alone. Tony Quade was there. Not only that, she thinks they were having an argument, but they stopped it when she came in."

"I can't believe even Bill Pagett would tell her she had to get an abortion in front of Tony Quade."

"You're absolutely right," said Bourke with sarcastic emphasis. "Pagett showed unsuspected sensitivity. He didn't mention an abortion, just talked to her for a bit and finally told her to go back home and that he'd see her the next night. But of course, he didn't, because he was dead."

"What was Tony Quade doing while all this was going on?"

"Pacing around drinking a can of beer. Pagett was nice enough to drive Hilary home, and when they left the house, Quade was still there. She says he looked angry, but she doesn't know why. In the car, she started to ask Pagett about Sybil Quade, but when she did, he turned on her, so she shut up." Bourke shook his head. "Sybil Quade has been lying to us," he observed.

"Yes," said Carol.

Chapter Eight

"Mrs. Quade?" Bourke said. "Inspector Ashton has asked me to contact you. I'm afraid there are a few details to clear up, and it would be a help if you could be available this afternoon here at the Bellwhether police station. I've already asked Mrs. Farrell to have your lessons covered. Would you like me to send a car for you, or would you rather drive yourself?"

She said she would rather take her own car, agreed on two o'clock as the time, and slowly replaced the receiver.

"What was that about?" asked Terry, who had come into the empty staff room as she had been speaking.

"The police. They want to ask me some more questions."

Terry was bitterly hostile. "Oh, really? Didn't that blonde bitch ask you enough questions yesterday evening?" At her startled look he smiled with grim satisfaction. "Yes, Syb. I went round to your place, just to see if everything was all right. And who should I see arriving but Inspector Bloody Ashton."

"You're spying on me."

"I don't see you have any reason to be angry. At least I'm not lying to you the way you are to me. Why did you fob me off by saying you had a headache?"

"For God's sake, Terry! Why must you always want something from me? Why can't you leave me alone?"

Surprisingly, Terry's face softened. "Don't get hysterical, Syb. I know you're under pressure. I wouldn't say these things to you if I didn't love you."

"No, of course you wouldn't," she said, flooded with relief at the realization that he had no idea what had happened between herself and Carol. She suddenly felt immensely tired. "Terry, about tonight. . . ."

His black eyes met hers. "Yes."

She didn't have the energy to fight him. "I don't want to go out for dinner. I don't want to see anyone, or run the risk of reporters. . . ."

He smiled. "Ah, Syb, I'll look after you. Pick you up and take you back to my place, eh? Cook you a wonderful dinner."

She surrendered. "All right," she said.

* * * * *

117

Carol looked formidably cool and efficient. "Would you sit down," she said formally. Bourke gave Sybil a slight smile, reminding her of the first interview after Bill's death. But it wasn't the same. They both knew so much more about her now, about her private life, about her feelings. She lifted her chin and returned Carol's look but it was Bourke who asked the first question.

"There seem to be some discrepancies in what you say and other reports we have received," he said.

"Could you give me a specific example?"

How cool you are, thought Carol.

Bourke continued, "You said you didn't see Bill Pagett on Sunday, the night before his death. We have a witness who says you did. What's more, we have information to suggest you had a violent argument with him."

Sybil sat silent. Pride is everything, she thought. The ancient Greeks looked at things the right way — it's how you face disaster that's important, not what happens afterwards.

"Would you like to comment?" asked Bourke.

"No."

"You do have the right to legal representation if you feel it's necessary," said Carol.

"It's not necessary."

"Do you deny being at Bill Pagett's house on Sunday night?" asked Bourke.

"No."

"You also stated that you hadn't seen your husband since he returned to Australia, but we are informed that he was present that evening. Is that true?"

"No."

"Are you saying you didn't see him?" asked Carol.

118

"I didn't know Tony was there — if he was." Sybil stood, and Bourke rose also. Sybil wondered fleetingly if he thought she was going to do something violent. She wished she could, just to release the spring of tension that was wound to breaking point. "I don't have to answer any of these questions, do I?" she said in a voice of polite inquiry.

Bourke looked thoughtful. "If you choose not to, Mrs. Quade, then that's your decision. However, your answers might be of considerable help to our investigations."

"I'm sorry I wasn't able to be of more help," said Sybil. She hesitated for a moment, then walked quickly out of the room.

Bourke flicked the pages of his notebook. "We've got to get more out of her than that," he said. He grinned at Carol. "Do you want me to make a house call? Use the famous Bourke charm?"

Carol was playing with a silver pen, turning it over and over in her fingers. "No, Mark. I'll give it another go myself."

Bourke shook his head. "It's going to break my heart if she's guilty," he said.

* * * * *

Sybil expected her, but when she saw the car draw up in the drive her pulse still leaped in fear and excitement. She opened the door to Carol's impatient knock and stood aside to let her in.

Carol flung down her briefcase on a couch and strode to the open windows. She took a deep breath and turned to Sybil. "Now's the time to stop lying, Sybil. It's too dangerous to worry about your feelings any more."

"I can't help you. Nothing that happened has anything to do with Bill's death. I didn't kill him. I don't know who did."

Carol's voice was tight with rage. "Can't you see. . . ." She threw up her hands. "Sybil, you look more guilty every time another crack appears in your story. You can keep repeating you're innocent all the way to Mulawa Women's Prison, if you like. I happen to think it would be a lot easier if you just told me the truth."

"There's nothing to say."

"Just tell me."

Sybil's eyes filled with furious tears. "And everything I tell you goes into a report, doesn't it? For people to read and snicker over. How would you like it? I don't suppose you've ever felt like I do. I hate the idea of people peering into my life." She gave an angry laugh. "The well-known invasion of privacy, Carol. I can't stand it."

"Tell me. I'll only put into my report what I have to."

"And I'm supposed to trust you?"

The anger faded from Carol's direct gaze. "You've got to trust someone, sometime. It might as well be me."

Sybil stared at her. Is it easier to trust beautiful people? she thought irrelevantly. I want to lean on you and ask you to help me. Aloud she said, "What do you want to know?"

"What was your real relationship with Bill Pagett?"

Sybil sat down so she could look out at the sea. "I hated him."

Having said that, there was no point in holding back. She continued calmly, "Bill was Tony's best friend. As I told you, the first time I met Tony was at Bill's place. And Bill was everything he admired — member of a famous family, up with all the political gossip, popular with

120

everyone, outstandingly successful with girls . . . Tony thought he was wonderful."

"Was there any suggestion of any sexual attraction between them?"

"No, there wasn't anything like that. It was the good old Aussie mateship in operation, at the expense of everything else."

"At the expense of your marriage?"

"As long as I behaved as a wife should, there was no reason to expect any trouble. You know how it is, Carol, indulging them — letting boys be boys."

"I know," said Carol.

Caught by her tone, Sybil said, "Have you been married?"

"Yes."

"Divorced?"

"Yes. Go on about Pagett."

"Bill didn't approve of the way I behaved. For one thing, I fought against changing my name. It wasn't Bill's ridicule that made me give in, but Tony, who said it was very important to him. Afterwards, I was sorry I agreed, but I decided it wasn't worth making a fuss." She smiled without humor. "It seems the easy way, doesn't it, to give in? Now I know it's weak and stupid. Even if you lose, at least you can say you tried."

"Did you and Bill Pagett openly argue?"

"Of course not. On the surface it was all in good fun. He used to call me a randy little bitch, just joking, of course, but I knew he was serious."

"Would many people know he used that term?"

"You're thinking of the phone calls, of course. He often said it when others were around, but always with a kind of affectionate charm. I think Bill and I were the only ones who knew what he really meant."

"Which was?"

"That he wanted me to know he thought I was like all the rest — just to be used. Women were fair game. If they cooperated and played along with him, he was happy. If they didn't, there was something wrong with them." Sybil began to pace up and down. "Carol, I don't think many people would agree with me over Bill. Almost everyone liked him."

"He told Florrie Dunstane that you had fallen in love with him."

"What else did he say?" said Sybil bitterly.

"In essence, that you threw yourself at him and he had to gently refuse you because of his friendship with your husband."

"How typically Bill," said Sybil contemptuously.

"Why did you write that note to him?"

"I was a fool, wasn't I? It was when I still thought I could, or should, save my marriage — that I still owed something to Tony. Bill got me alone, called to see me when Tony was out. I was a challenge to him, a woman who didn't melt when he felt her up — all in fun, of course." She swung around. "Bill was so much fun!" she said bitingly.

"What happened?"

"He put the hard word on me. I don't think he could believe I wouldn't give in to him if he really tried. And I think he wanted Tony to come home and find us together. It was horrible. He tried to physically force me . . . and then we both heard Tony driving in. Suddenly he was back to the usual charming Bill. I didn't trust him. I didn't want him to think that afterwards I'd say anything to Tony, because if he did, he'd concoct some story to say I'd made the first move. I suppose I knew Tony would believe him rather than me. Now, I can't understand why I bothered, but it was important then, important to make sure Tony didn't suspect anything."

"Why write a note? Why not ring him?"

"I don't know if you'll understand. I hated him so much I couldn't bear to speak to him. But I had to stop him from saying anything, so I wrote that note and then drove over to slip it under his door. It was such a stupid thing to do. It just gave him ammunition to use against me."

"The night before Bill Pagett died — why did you go to see him if you couldn't stand him?"

Sybil sighed. "Bill rang me and said he'd heard from Tony, and that he was returning to Australia. I didn't want him back, I didn't want to have to face him. Bill said Tony was tossing up whether to return or not, that it depended on me. He said we'd have to discuss it face to face. I didn't want to go, but I couldn't just leave it. Finally I said I'd call over. He was alone. I didn't see Tony, but you said he was there. Was that true?"

"Hilary Cosgrove was outside. She's one of your students, isn't she? It seems she and Pagett were lovers. She saw you leave, couldn't decide what to do, so started to walk home, then she changed her mind and went back. She said your husband was there with Pagett."

"So Tony could have arrived while she was starting to walk home? He might not have actually been there when Bill. . . ."

"When Bill what?" Carol looked at her expression. "Sybil, it's all right. Please tell me."

Sybil couldn't keep still. She shook off Carol's hand, walking around the room, touching things, looking unseeingly out at the view, while Carol sat silently watching her. "How can I explain to you how I feel, Carol? I've always hidden any feelings of hurt, embarrassment or anger, even when I was a child. It's important to me to keep face — to seem to be in control — not to be at a disadvantage. Do you understand?"

"I do, but there are times when you have to run the risk of exposing how you feel."

Sybil nodded, resigned. "Do you know what Bill did to me, Carol, or rather, tried to do? Rape me. He wasn't trying to kiss me, or persuade me. He wanted to humiliate me. Teach me a lesson by raping me. He didn't bother to pretend to discuss Tony, just shoved me back against a table. And all the time he was telling me he knew I really wanted it. Let me ram it up you, he kept on saying. And when I resisted, he slapped me, hard. I couldn't escape: he was stronger than I was."

"What happened?"

"I hit him with a glass ashtray, on the side of the jaw. I got away from him and I screamed at him. I lost all my precious control, Carol. I picked up anything I could and threw it at him. And then I ran." She looked down at her hands. "Not very edifying, is it?" She gave a twisted smile. "And maybe Tony was there, listening."

"What did you do when you left?"

"I went home and cried. Cried over bastards like them. It makes me sick to think about it."

"And nothing else?"

"Oh, you want to know if I went home and practiced with my Black and Decker? Sorry, Carol, I hate to disappoint you."

"Sybil, I have to ask these questions."

"Sure you do."

Carol put her hand out. "I understand. . . ."

"Do you?" Sybil was bitter. "Do you? You think you know what makes me tick?" She swung around in sudden

124

fury. "Carol, I hate what you make me feel! I don't want to care about you! I don't want. . . ."

The electricity of passion flickered between them.

"No, don't," said Carol as Sybil put her arms around her. Tongue to tongue, heart to heart, thought Carol, holding Sybil's head with both hands and kissing her ardently, abandoning for a moment the restraint that she had promised herself. Then she pulled away. "No," she said again.

Sybil's eyes were unfocused with desire. "It frightens me," she said, "I've never felt this way before."

"In the circumstances, it sure scares the hell out of me, too," said Carol with an attempt at humor. She watched with surprise as anger flared again on Sybil's face.

"Oh, I'm compromising your investigation am I? Are you afraid I'll go to the Commissioner and announce we're having an affair? Is that it? Or do you think I'll embarrass you in public, appear on Pierre Brand's show and say you seduced me?"

"I'm sure you won't do any of those things, but that isn't the point. I shouldn't be on this case, not the way I feel about you."

Sybil's face was wet with tears. "And how do you feel? Aroused?" she asked, her voice shaking. She looked at Carol's still face. "Get out, go away," she said.

"Sybil. . . ."

"Please. Just go away. Please."

And when Carol had gone, she cried in earnest, partly because of the resurrection of ugly memories, partly because she had told Carol to go, and Carol had obeyed her.

* * * * *

125

Carol slammed down the phone and groaned. "I have to give Pierre Brand an interview," she said to Bourke. "The Commissioner says it's an excellent idea and so does Sir Richard. Good for the image, I understand. Blonde Inspector expects early arrest, that sort of approach — bland, soothing and good PR. Of course, it's not good enough for Brand to send a reporter to an ordinary press conference — he must have an exclusive."

Bourke grunted sympathetically. "Going to the funeral?" he asked. "Looks like it'll be quite a show."

Carol made a face. "Yes, that's the other media duty. 'You look so good in black,' the Commissioner said to me, 'and Sir Richard expects you to be there.' So I'm practicing my pensive but resolute expression for the cameras."

"Tony Quade's funeral's tomorrow, too," said Bourke, "but in the morning at the Northern Suburbs Crematorium. Close friends only and no flowers. And I bet my favorite redhead, our Sybil, will also look stunning in black."

"Since you're going, you'll be able to see."

"Perhaps she'll break down and confess all, over the coffin," said Bourke. "After all, now we have her fingerprints on the baseball bat. Doesn't look too good for her, does it?"

"She gave you an explanation."

"Yes," said Bourke. "Every Wednesday she sends a kid to collect the baseball stuff from the teacher in charge of the PE equipment store. The student puts everything in her car because Bellwhether Oval is a fair way from the school. At the oval, she deals everything out, reversing the whole process at the end of the afternoon. But isn't it stretching things a bit to suppose that of the twelve baseball bats the school has, the very one used to kill

126

Tony Quade happens to have his wife's fingerprints on it?"

"They weren't on the handle."

"No, that was wiped clean. But how about this: Sybil whacks her husband across the head, pushes him over the cliff, wipes the handle of the bat and throws it down onto the ledge, completely forgetting in her haste that she may have touched other parts of it."

Carol looked dubious. "Why wasn't the bat found straight away?" she said.

"You think it was planted? Could be, but why?"

"Perhaps someone's going to a lot of trouble to make sure she's suspected — the phone calls, the note sent to us, the drill — it could be a setup."

"Yeah, or Sybil mightn't be as smart as she could be," said Bourke, rolling his eyes. "I mean, it doesn't seem fair if she's got looks and brains too, does it?"

"How are you going on 'randy little bitch' and 'ram it up her?' " said Carol abruptly.

"From what I can find out, randy was one of Pagett's favorite words, and he usually used it in a joking way. Even Florrie Dunstane remembers it fondly as one of Bill's amusing little references. As for the charming expression, ram it up her, I can't find anyone to admit that Pagett, or for that matter, anyone else, used it regularly. I suppose the wording could be a coincidence, though that's stretching it a bit."

"Any more on Witcombe?"

"Not much. Last June he was arrested for disturbing the peace outside a cinema showing an R-rated film with the usual bondage, rape and violence in it. The magistrate put him on a good behavior bond. He's a card-carrying member of the Family First movement and does his stint

127

in front of abortion clinics etcetera. Besides being to the far right of Goebbels, he seems okay."

"I'd like you to have a little chat with him, man to man. You know the approach — how the rot's set in, society's not the same, marriage under attack — that sort of thing. See if you can encourage him to talk. He might see himself as a one-man vigilante group, ridding the world of corruption."

"Somehow, Alan Witcombe doesn't strike me as an Australian Rambo," said Bourke, "but I must admit the idea has great entertainment potential, and wouldn't the media love it."

"I know Pierre Brand would," said Carol caustically.

Chapter Nine

Carol kicked off her shoes and sighed. It had been a long, hard day. Being serenely charming takes a lot out of you, she thought. And she hated funerals because they always reminded her of her parents' deaths. First her father, unexpectedly of a heart attack, and then her mother, gray and grieving, had surrendered to the cancer she had battled successfully for years. Her parents had had such a close marriage that neither could bear to be without the other. Would she ever have that comfort, that support, that happiness? She padded around, feeding the demands of her fat cat, pouring a drink and munching a handful of peanuts, postponing the telephone call she must make, not because she was reluctant to ring, but because she wanted to so much. It's part of your investigations, she said mockingly to herself — although it's not too obvious, Carol, why you just have to see her, alone, here. I won't ring her, she thought. I can interview her tomorrow.

She gulped down her drink, curled up on the couch, and dialed. The phone rang and rang. Finally the receiver was snatched up at the other end. "Yes?"

"It's Carol. Sybil?"

"Yes."

"Are you alone?"

"Yes."

"Do you want to come over here?" A pause. Carol chewed at a thumbnail. "Don't if you don't want to," she said. "You must be terribly tired. . . ."

"I want to come."

Carol was determinedly casual. "Okay. See you when I see you." She put down the phone and stared into space, absently stroking the cat who, ignoring the heat, had clambered onto her lap and was purring enthusiastically. "Pussy cat," she said to him, "why am I doing this? It can't work. She wouldn't be willing to pay the price."

When Sybil arrived her hair was wet and her face scrubbed and shining. "After the funeral I went for a swim, way out, past the breakers. I looked back at the beach and the headlands, and they seemed so far away . . . I was sorry when I had to swim back in." Suddenly she felt shy and awkward. Did that sound like she was asking for sympathy?

Carol smiled at her. "Would you like to sit on the deck? I've got a coil burning to discourage the mosquitos, and the sunset is still spectacular."

I haven't felt like this since I was a kid, thought Sybil. Aloud she said, "Sorry I took so long to answer the phone. I was under the shower, and anyway, I thought it was Terry, and so I didn't hurry."

"Have you eaten yet?" said Carol. "No? Neither have I. I'll get some wine and something light to eat." Pausing in the doorway, she watched Sybil sit in the deep wooden chair and throw her head back to watch the treetops dancing against the rockmelon orange sky. "You mentioned Terry Clarke. . . ."

"We had dinner last night. And of course he was at Tony's funeral." There was irony in her tone as she added, "Supporting the grieving widow."

"Were you upset?"

"I was sad, because someone was dead. I hadn't seen Tony for months. . . ." Her mind leaped to the scene in the morgue: "When I identified him, it was just his body — it wasn't Tony. Besides, when we separated, in a way I said goodbye for good. Today, at the funeral, there didn't seem to be any connection to the person I married."

Carol excused herself to go to the kitchen. Sybil sat in the fading light, gazing out at the still water and thinking about the evening before.

As he had promised, Terry had picked her up after school and taken her back to his flat. He was a capable if not inspired cook, and he had served a reasonable Italian dish. Sybil remembered staring at him while they ate, trying to imagine making love to him. A thick mat of black hair showed at the collar of his shirt, and she knew from

131

the beach that his back was similarly covered. She compared Carol's smooth body, and was fired with a pulse of desire. I'm not like that, she said to herself, rejecting the image.

"Syb? You're not listening," Terry said.

"Sorry."

"Of course, it's the funeral tomorrow. Don't worry, I'll be there with you."

Terry's barely disguised passion for her was somehow reassuring. It meant she was still a paid-up member of the normal majority. With clinical detachment she watched her own actions and reactions. She deliberately drank several glasses of wine with dinner, which, combined with the two whiskeys she'd had earlier, began to impart a pleasant fuzzy glow. After dinner she accepted a glass of port with her coffee, and was distantly amused at the large amount Terry poured her. He's trying to get me drunk, she thought, so the big seduction scene is coming up.

She was viewing everything from a point some distance away. I'm smashed, she thought. She watched Terry sit beside her, slide an arm along the back of the sofa, put his other hand on her knee. I am feeling some stirrings of physical desire, aren't I? she asked herself. She tried to concentrate. Terry was saying something about how he felt, about how much he wanted her. Then he was kissing her. In her alcoholic haze she thought of Carol's tongue in her mouth, and immediately her body responded. Terry's caresses grew more urgent, his arousal greater. Oh God, thought Sybil, why not? She despised the sexual tease. I might even enjoy it, she remembered saying to herself.

"Do you want a light on?" said Carol, handing her a plate of salad and a fork.

Sybil was startled by the return of the present. "Thanks," she said automatically, then, as Carol seated herself she blurted out, "I slept with Terry Clarke last night."

It was now so dark she couldn't see Carol's face clearly, and her voice was noncommittal. "Oh?"

Sybil exhaled a long breath. "I don't know why I told you that," she said.

"Yes you do."

There was a pause. "Why?" said Sybil at last.

"Because you want me to know you're a normal, heterosexual woman, with all the correct feelings and reactions."

"Carol, it wasn't . . . maybe it was for something like that, but it was to prove something to *me,* not to you."

Carol's silver voice was cool. "Do you want some wine?"

"No. That was the trouble last night. I was drunk."

"Oh? You have to be drunk to have sex with a man? Doesn't that worry you a bit, Sybil?" said Carol sarcastically.

"Yes, it does. And it also worries me that all the time he was making love to me I was thinking of you. And that every time I remembered what we did together my body responded."

Silence. A slight breeze blew from the water and Sybil could smell the scent of jasmine. Summer breeze, makes me feel fine, she thought, the music running in her mind. "Carol, I don't understand why I feel this way."

"When your marriage was at its best . . . did you have a good sexual relationship?"

The darkness made it easy to answer. "The sex was all right, nothing wonderful, but okay. I've never expected that much from physical love, anyway." That needed more explanation: "I grew up the same as everyone else. Sex was automatic once you were going steady with some guy. I was a bit disappointed, I suppose — I expected too much, but it wasn't unpleasant. And with Tony it was better than most."

"So the earth didn't move for you on a regular basis?" said Carol.

"It does when I'm with you."

The silence lengthened. "Well, that's a conversation stopper," Carol said at last.

"I want to sleep with you," said Sybil before caution could prevent her. "I want us to make love, and then sleep together." Her words hung in the air between them. "Carol?"

"It's a comparison you want, is it Sybil? Last night Terry Clarke and tonight Carol Ashton? And what are you going to prove, to yourself or anyone else?"

"It's not like that."

Carol was remorseless. "Or perhaps you have another motive altogether? Could it be that you think I'll protect you, not arrest you, no matter how guilty you are, if you have an emotional and physical hold over me?"

"Oh, come on, Carol!"

"This is your cue to say you really love me, that you can't live without me. Are you going to say that, Sybil?"

"No, I'm not going to say that."

Carol put out an arm to restrain her, but Sybil flung it away, snatched up her things and ran out of the house. She didn't remember driving home: all the way the evening ran like a continuous loop in her imagination — Carol's voice, the nuances of words, and most of all the disturbing excitement of the emotions that had vibrated between them.

"Carol?" said Bourke. "Sorry to ring you so late, but I've just got home from a cup of coffee with Florrie and Lionel Dunstane, and there are a couple of things I though you'd like to know."

"What did you get?"

"Coffee and a piece of cake."

"Mark, I'm not in the mood for humor."

"Well, Lionel Dunstane's bedridden, of course, so apart from radio and television, he relies on Florrie's little snippets of gossip. That made it easy to get them chatting about Bellwhether High, and the two of them rambled on for an hour or so."

"Mark, will you get on with it?"

"Oh, sorry, am I interrupting something?" At Carol's irritated sigh, he said hastily, "Well, the first thing is that not only does Terry Clarke make a habit of shadowing Sybil Quade in his car to check where she goes and who she sees, but he had a particular reason to be interested in her movements the Sunday night before Pagett died. It seems that Pete McIvor was on Bellwhether Beach on Sunday morning when Clarke and Pagett practically had a stand-up fight over the redhead I most admire. Apparently Pagett announced that he and Sybil had a date that night, which didn't please Terry Clarke at all. Pagett's last words were something in the order of 'Don't hang around Syb's place waiting to see her, she's spending the night with me.' Actually I think Florrie was sparing my feelings — I suspect the words were rather more basic, but that was the general message. Clarke threatened him and left. End of story."

"Why do you think Pete McIvor has conveniently forgotten to mention this argument?"

"Who knows?" said Bourke. "Maybe it's misplaced loyalty, although frankly I think he's frightened Terry Clarke will tear his head off if he says anything."

"We'll follow it up tomorrow. What else?"

"One of Florrie's duties is to sort the mail coming into the school. She was delighted to tell me that Mrs. Farrell has received a series of letters identical to the one you got, each in a square white envelope with 'personal and private' printed in sloping capital letters."

"Is she sure they were the same?"

"Absolutely. For one thing, very little mail to Bellwhether is marked as personal. And you must take into account Florrie's lively interest in everything around her. I think what particularly impressed her about the letters was the effect they had on Mrs. Farrell."

"Which was?"

"Barely restrained shock — God-not-again, but mustn't let the staff see me clutch at my throat — sort of reaction."

"Colorful," said Carol. "They were Florrie's exact words?"

"Of course not. I like to add a little zip to my reports."

"Any idea when Mrs. Farrell received the last one?"

"On Thursday, the day Quade's body was discovered at the bottom of the cliff."

"She's positive it was Thursday last week?"

"She is. She says the second death burned the events of that day into her mind," said Mark with amusement, "and those *were* her exact words."

"It'll be interesting to hear what Mrs. Farrell has to say. I'll leave it to you to ring and suggest we see her early tomorrow in her office."

"Do you want to hear about my man-to-man meeting with Alan Witcombe?"

"Can it wait till tomorrow?"

"Sure . . . Carol, you sound tired. Are you okay?"

"I'm fine. I'll see you tomorrow."

Chapter Ten

Carol was wearing a green that exactly matched the color of her eyes. Bourke looked at her admiringly as she walked through the main doors of Bellwhether High's administration block. "You look great this morning," he said.

She gave him a brief smile. "Mrs. Farrell?" she said.

"Mrs. Farrell's been called away — some kid's fallen off the Art Block roof while trying to get a ball. I get the impression the Education Department demands reports in triplicate with twenty witnesses, but she says she won't be long. She said to make ourselves comfortable in her office, but I don't know if she really meant it. There's a certain frosty reserve about our Mrs. Farrell this morning."

"Perhaps she knows why we're here," said Carol as she entered the principal's office. She looked at the green carpet and pale furniture, and visualized Sybil the first time she had seen her. "Tell me about Witcombe," she said, sitting down.

"Before I describe the fascinating two hours I had with him, just let me tell you about Evan Berry. You asked me to find out if he knew about Hilary's pregnancy. Well, the answer seems to be no. There was no way Hilary wanted Evan or anyone else to know about it. She only told her parents after Pagett was killed."

"So Evan doesn't have a real motive."

"No, and he doesn't seem the type to plan such a careful murder — he'd be the impulsive, oh-God-what've-I-done sort."

"I hope you're using less racy language in your reports," observed Carol. "Now, about Alan Witcombe. . . ."

Bourke had found it easy to get Alan Witcombe to talk once he had innocently commented upon the present and future degradation of society. Alan was delighted to discuss corruption, both in broad terms and in specifics. Bourke introduced the problem of immorality among teachers and the influence this could have upon students, and had been rewarded with a much more detailed picture of Bellwhether High's staff than that which Carol had obtained from him.

"Don't be upset," said Bourke with a grin. "Alan Witcombe wouldn't discuss these sorts of things with a lady like yourself."

Witcombe had made moral judgments on his colleagues with some enthusiasm. He had found Bill Pagett a disgrace to the profession of teaching, but was well aware there was no way he could do anything without proof. Unfortunately, while there was a good supply of rumor and innuendo about Bill Pagett, no one was willing to come forward with details of times and places. He was sure Pagett had had a bad influence on Pete McIvor by encouraging him to gamble in illegal casinos, but his fatherly words to Pete had been ignored. He had a high opinion of Edwina, although he deplored the viciousness of her tongue at times. Did Bourke know that she, single-handed, looked after an invalid mother? About Lynne he had some reservations. Bourke privately thought Lynne would represent a painted woman to Alan's biblical eyes. Certainly she seemed to be a good mother, but he had the impression that she indulged in a succession of relationships. Bourke delicately referred to the mention of nymphomania Florrie had repeated. Alan frowned at this. It was a word seriously misused and one which was bandied around far too freely. In Lynne's case he was sure it wouldn't apply. She was ultimately looking for a permanent relationship, he thought, but perhaps she was searching in the wrong area. Bourke wondered if that meant Alan thought she should join Family First.

"What about Terry Clarke?" said Carol.

"Witcombe said he was the brooding Heathcliff type." He made a face. "Who was Heathcliff?" he said.

"A tormented, jealous, romantic hero," said Carol, amused. "Terry Clarke cast as the Heathcliff of Bellwhether High. Well, well. Alan Witcombe has a sense of humor after all."

"And," said Bourke as Mrs. Farrell came into view, "Alan thinks Sybil Quade is wonderful. Not a word against her. I find that suspicious in itself, don't you?"

* * * * *

"Thank God it's Friday," said Pete McIvor to the staff room in general.

Edwina, resplendent in yellow, was in a waspish mood. "I don't know what's worn you out, Pete — it certainly wouldn't be teaching."

"What's that supposed to mean?"

"It means, Peter dear," said Edwina with an edge in her voice, "that your distinct lack of effort has been noticed. I happen to know you didn't bother to do either of your playground duties, and I'm getting sick and tired of disciplining your classes for you. Every time there's a racket from your room, I go in — and where's little Peter? Not there." She glared at him. "And stop stroking your bloody mustache, will you? Did you grow it to prove you have balls?"

Pete's fair skin flushed. "Look, the cops wanted to see me. It's not my fault there wasn't someone covering my classes."

"And what did they want to see you about?" asked Lynne lazily as she painted a fingernail blood red.

"Something about sports equipment. The stuff we use for softball and baseball."

"Tsk, tsk," said Edwina, "I detect the noose tightening about Syb's neck, don't you?"

Pete looked appalled. "Syb? Are you saying they think she killed Bill?"

"And her husband," added Edwina. "Of course, I'm sure Syb's not guilty, but it's starting to look awfully bad for her."

"I don't see what sports have got to do with it."

"Of course you don't, Pete. You've never been the brightest boy on the block, have you?" Edwina beamed at him. "I think you'll find that Bill, to make him more amenable to having a hole drilled in his head, was knocked out by something rather like a bat. And funnily enough, a kid in my roll class, Bruce Kennedy, happened to spill the fact that he'd found a school baseball bat up on the headland where Tony Quade took a dive." Her smile widened. "Looks incriminating for you, too, Pete. I mean, you supervise baseball with Syb on Wednesday afternoons, don't you? Gives you a great chance to take some of the equipment. Who knows, maybe you and Syb are in it together . . . though I would have thought she'd have chosen more wisely."

Pete's face was now beetroot as he struggled to find a rejoinder. Lynne interposed lazily, "Leave him alone, Edwina, will you?" She yawned. "Speaking of Syb, do you happen to know if Pierre Brand got her to cooperate?"

Edwina shrugged her yellow shoulders. "Frankly, I think Syb's decided to tough it out."

"Tough what out?" demanded Terry, who had walked in as Edwina had been speaking. "What are you saying about Syb?"

"My, Terry, you did look good on television," said Edwina, ignoring his question. "And Syb looked ravishing, as usual. But do you think it was wise to go to the funeral with her? People could talk, and the last thing she needs is a motive, I'm sure you'll agree."

"God, you're a poisonous bitch," he said.

"And I love you, too," Edwina replied with amusement.

"Where is Syb, anyway?" said Lynne, inspecting her nail polish at the window. "Don't tell me our paragon of virtue is going to be late *again*. That would make it twice this week — quite a record for someone so punctual."

Lynne appeared not at all put out to hear Sybil say, "Thanks, Lynne. It's nice to know you're taking such a keen interest in my activities."

"How did it go with Pierre Brand?" Lynne said.

"I haven't spoken to him. Why?"

"Oh, just that he was very keen to interview you. He thought you got the wrong idea the other day at Edwina's."

"What wrong idea was that?" asked Sybil tightly.

Lynne made an expansive gesture. "Syb! You can't beat them, so you might as well join them. Cooperate with Pierre and you'll get a fair coverage, but you know what he's like if he decides to dissect someone on his program."

"I'm not going to talk to him."

"Suit yourself, Syb," said Lynne, "but don't say I didn't warn you."

There's no point in arguing, thought Sybil, turning away to put her things on her desk. She felt tears sting her eyes. I'm tired and depressed and if Terry touches me I'll scream.

"Coming to assembly?" said Terry, putting his arm loosely around her shoulders.

"Okay," said Sybil, postponing the scream and hunting for dark glasses in her purse. She waited until they were walking together to the assembly area to say, "Terry, don't touch me, all right? I just don't want to give them any ammunition — you know how people talk."

143

"Let them. I'm going to look after you, Syb. Don't let things get you down."

"Hah," said Sybil without mirth.

* * * * *

Mrs. Farrell didn't take the assembly as she usually did — that task fell to her deputy principal. Instead she sat looking across her desk at Carol Ashton's expression of polite inquiry. Mrs. Farrell cleared her throat. "I suppose you're wondering why I didn't mention these letters before?" she said.

"Yes," said Carol.

Bourke filled the awkward pause: "You say you've received a total of five letters?"

"Yes, and I'm afraid I've destroyed them all, except for the last one." She straightened her shoulders. "Inspector, if you look at it from my point of view, these scurrilous letters deserved to be consigned to the waste paper basket. To do anything else was to dignify them with some kind of weight."

"Have you the last one with you?"

Mrs. Farrell unlocked the top drawer of her desk and drew out a square white envelope. Handling it as though it were contaminated, she passed it to Carol. "You must realize I had no idea that they were anything else but nuisance letters, designed to give some sick person a cheap thrill."

"But if they were making allegations about your staff, surely they were worth reporting officially?"

Mrs. Farrell tightened her mouth. "It was my judgment not to do so."

144

Carol handed the letter to Bourke, who opened it with the help of tweezers. "We have your fingerprints, Mrs. Farrell?" said Carol.

"You do," said Mrs. Farrell, remembering with distaste the ink and the familiar way the constable had pressed her fingers down to obtain the prints.

The single sheet of paper had been folded to fit the envelope exactly and it was written in the same sloping capitals as the address:

Phyllis darling,

Don't you think his eyes should have been out? Drilled out his eyes to stop him looking at those young girls. Still, now that Bill won't be ramming it up that randy bitch Sybil Quade or any teenage girls anymore think you should turn your attention to the head of English have you noticed how Alan smacks his lips when he talks about sex and he talks about it all the time and it's not just girls he feels the boys up too watch him you just watch him he gets an erection just thinking about sin.

"Tsk," said Bourke, "and it isn't even signed A Friend."

Mrs. Farrell didn't smile. "The others were very much in the same vein," she said. "I suppose you want details?"

"I suppose we do," said Carol.

* * * * *

"Alan?"

Witcombe looked up from his office desk at Sybil's voice. "Syb, you look dreadful. Come in and sit down."

145

"Alan, I'm sorry, I think I have to go home."

"Syb, you shouldn't have come to school today. The funeral must have been a strain."

"I've got a senior class this afternoon and a junior English before lunch booked in to see a video on Dickens. I know it's inconvenient, but I really can't face them. Is there any way you can cover them for me?"

"Of course, don't worry about it." He leaned forward. "Syb, how are you coping? Are you all right alone, particularly at night?"

Sybil thought of how much she wanted Carol's company. "I'm okay," she said to Alan.

"I tried to ring you last night, but you didn't answer. Thought you must have gone out."

As head of the English Department, Alan had her unlisted number as a matter of course, but he had only contacted her a couple of times in the last year, and then early in the morning about school matters. "Why were you ringing me?" she said.

"Just to see how you felt — if there was anything Alice or I could do to help. We wondered if you'd like to stay with us until this whole thing's over."

Sybil felt close to tears at this unexpected kindness. "Alan, that's so thoughtful of you both. Actually I was out — Inspector Ashton asked to see me."

Alan looked stern. "Such a pity," he said, "I had a lot of time for the Inspector, until I found out she was an unfit mother."

"What?"

"It's been kept quiet, of course, but she has a son, and when she and her husband divorced, she freely gave up custody. Unnatural behavior for a mother, I'm sure you'll agree."

"Unnatural behavior," repeated Sybil.

146

"Children should be with their mothers. Ideally, of course, they should be with both parents, but I'm not unrealistic, I know some marriages aren't perfect, so divorce is an unpleasant necessity." He looked concerned. "Syb, I wasn't referring to you and Tony . . . your separation. . . ."

"It's okay, I know you weren't. You were saying about Carol Ashton. . . ."

"It just so happens that through the Family First meetings, I've come in contact with some legal men, top of the profession, concerned about the way society is going . . . well, the other night we were having a cup of coffee after the meeting and the conversation turned to the dreadful things happening here at Bellwhether. I found myself talking to a close friend of Inspector Ashton's ex-husband, and he was saying how she just walked out on her marriage, left her son, and refused to have anything more to do with her husband, Justin Hart. You must know his name, he's a very well-known barrister." He shook his head. "Apparently she didn't change her name when she married him." Alan's expression indicated that he thought the rot had set in from that point.

Sybil said. "We don't know the whole story. Maybe there's a reason she didn't ask for custody."

Alan looked dubious. "Syb, I can't think of one reason why a normal, natural mother wouldn't want to be with her child. Can you?" When she remained silent he said, "I shouldn't be keeping you here. Go home, I'll make sure your classes are okay. And Syb, try and get away from Sydney this weekend. I'm sure you'll feel better if you do."

* * * * *

147

As soon as Sybil got home she went to the telephone. "Is Inspector Ashton there?"

"May I ask who's calling?"

"Sybil Quade."

A pause, and then a jolt at Carol's voice: "Yes, Mrs. Quade?"

"This is an official call," said Sybil, feeling ridiculous.

"Yes, of course."

"You're not much help," said Sybil.

The silver voice seemed faintly amused. "No."

"Is someone else there with you?"

"That's right."

Sybil wondered if Carol really was restricted by someone else's presence, or if she just didn't want to speak to her at a personal level. She felt ridiculously uncertain and embarrassed as she said, "It's about. . . . Well, I want to go away this weekend — out of Sydney. I thought . . . perhaps you should know, officially, that is."

"Where will you be going?"

"To the Far North Coast — Grafton."

"That's a long way for a weekend."

"Carol, I've got to get away. I can't stay here. My friend Barbara — probably my best friend — she moved up there last year — escaping the city, that sort of thing."

"You'll be flying, of course. When will you be leaving?"

"Tomorrow morning. I've tentatively booked a flight. So it's all right then?"

"Just give me details so we can contact you if we need to."

Sybil gave her the information, then waited, angry with herself because she was reluctant to hang up.

"You'll be at your usual address until tomorrow morning?" said Carol.

148

Sybil's heart leaped. "Carol, I'll be alone. No one will be here."

She waited. Carol said, "Yes, that's interesting. Thank you for calling."

The moment she replaced the receiver, the phone rang again. "Oh, hello Terry . . . I'm sorry I didn't see you before I left school . . . No, I'm not sick, I've just had enough . . . I'm going away for the weekend . . . Barbara's. I'm flying up tomorrow morning. . . . Thanks, but I'll leave my car at the airport. It's easier when I get back to have it there. . . . No, I don't want to see you tonight. Please, Terry, will you just for once take no for an answer?"

Terry was implacable. She was still arguing fruitlessly against his smug proprietary tone that drove her mad with irritation when to her relief she heard the front doorbell sound. "Terry, sorry, I've got to go because there's someone at the door. Call you when I get back on Sunday night, okay?"

The caller was hardly more welcome than Terry's telephone call. "Mrs. Quade, I saw you at your husband's funeral, but of course I didn't want to intrude."

"How thoughtful of you, Mr. Brand. I gather you considered your television cameras and crew weren't an intrusion?"

Pierre Brand gave an appropriately regretful smile. "I am always worried about the problems of privacy versus the public's right to know," he said smoothly.

Sybil had no intention of allowing him into the house. "I'm sorry," she said, "but you've called at a very inconvenient time. If you don't mind. . . ."

"Inspector Ashton has let drop to me, unofficially, of course, that you are the main suspect in this rather bizarre case. I wonder if you'd like to comment on this?"

149

He was standing to one side as he spoke, and Sybil caught a glimpse of reflected light from a car parked across the road. "You're filming this," she said.

"Would you like to say anything about the murders — for example, about your interesting relationships with both victims?"

All her anger and frustration boiled over. "I'd like to push you down the steps!" she exclaimed.

He smiled at her, delighted. "Do you always respond so violently, Mrs. Quade?"

She didn't trust herself to say anything else, so she stepped back and slammed the door. She leaned her forehead against the wood. "Why did I say that?"

She was puzzled to hear Pierre Brand's voice in conversation on the other side of the door. Then she realized what he was doing — delivering the Pierre Brand on-site monologue to tie up the story. She had watched his shows where shonky business people, con-artists and the shocked victims of crime had been given the Pierre Brand specialty — the knock at the door, the charming smile, the questions designed to confuse, annoy or confront, followed by Brand turning to the camera with some concluding words that usually skated just close enough to libel to titillate his audience but kept him out of court — all this lovingly caught on videotape, carefully edited, and presented to a public primed to receive the latest scandal delivered in easy-to-digest but sensational television morsels.

As she stood irresolute, his voice stopped, then, after a moment, a white card was pushed under the door. She stared at it, then picked it up. On his business card Pierre Brand had written in tiny, spidery writing: *Suggest to your distinct advantage to let us put to air your side of the*

*story right now, before you're arrested. Then, it'll be too
late for both of us.*

She carefully placed the card face down on the
television set. What had he said to her? That Carol had
told him, unofficially, that she was the main suspect. Did
Carol really believe that she could coldbloodedly kill two
people?

* * * * *

"The detailed lab report on the stuff vacuumed up in
Pagett's workroom has just arrived," said Bourke.
"Haven't had time to read it yet."

Carol took it and began to skim read. "Look at this,
Mark! Those flakes of colored lacquer mentioned in the
preliminary report have been identified as nail polish."

Bourke looked over her shoulder. "Pale pink pearl
nail varnish," he read from the page. "How would flakes
of nail polish get on the floor? Chipped fingernails?"

"I imagine so. Of course, there might not be any
connection with Pagett's murder."

Bourke grinned. "In these enlightened times the girls
do woodwork with the real men," he said. "There must be
a chipped fingernail or two — a small price to pay for
equality, I say."

"Perhaps it'll wipe the grin off your face to learn I
want to know which of the suspects wore nail polish on
the morning of the murder — and, of course, if any had
chipped nails."

Looking rather less enthusiastic, Bourke said, "We
know Lynne Simpson always wears nail polish. Won't she
do? It'll save a lot of trouble if we just arrest her, won't
it?"

"I've only noticed her wearing deep red colors."

151

Bourke nodded. "Yeah, I remember thinking in the first interview with her that her nails looked like they were dipped in blood. Horrible purple-red color."

Carol said, "Pale pink's the sort of color a young girl might wear, isn't it?"

"Well, I'll certainly check out Hilary Cosgrove, though I don't expect many people will remember a little detail like nail color."

"And this doesn't rule out the male suspects," said Carol. "It may be a red herring."

"More like a pale pink pearl herring," said Bourke, his humor restored.

* * * * *

Somehow Sybil had to fill in time until she could escape to Barbara's friendship. She wrote a neat list and stuck it to the refrigerator, thinking with a wry smile that anxiety had made her outstandingly efficient. Following its instructions, she packed her suitcase for the trip tomorrow, arranged for the neighbors to feed Jeffrey and then cleaned the house, changed the bed, tidied the cupboards — anything to keep occupied. She usually turned the radio up high while she ironed or did the housework, singing along with favorite songs, executing a dance step or two, mimicking the commercials she knew well, but today she needed silence. She felt as if sandpaper had been used on her nerves so that any loud noise would be an assault.

She jumped at the sound of the knock, but was elaborately casual when she answered the door. "Hi. Come in."

Carol looked tired and drawn. "Sybil, I'm sorry about last night."

152

"I don't suppose I helped by bringing up Terry, and then storming out like someone in a soap opera, did I?"

"Forget it?" said Carol.

"Forget it," agreed Sybil, handing Carol Pierre Brand's card. "He was here this afternoon. Had someone filming while he talked. I lost my temper and said something stupid. Later he shoved this under the door."

"How would he know you were home? He would expect you to still be at school."

Sybil rubbed her forehead. "I don't know, maybe he follows me around like Terry does."

Carol glanced at the card. "I think someone at your school rang him." Her face didn't change as she read the card. Handing it back, she said, "He's trying to scare you into an interview, that's all."

"I could be on his show tonight."

Carol smiled. "You'll be in good company. I recorded an interview with him earlier today."

Keeping her voice neutral, Sybil said, "He told me you said, unofficially, I was the main suspect."

"I didn't say anything like that at all. He was trying to frighten you into saying something stupid."

Sybil made a face. "Well, I fulfilled his wildest dreams."

"Perhaps we'd better watch his show."

Sybil was disconcerted by Carol's cool reserve, but what did she expect? A warm hug? A kiss? She escaped to the kitchen to make coffee. Returning, she said, "Carol?" The green eyes met hers. Say you love me, she thought. Aloud she said, "Do you take sugar in your coffee?"

Carol stood up and stretched. "No, just black, thanks. Sybil, does Terry Clarke really follow you around? I mean, shadow you in his car — that sort of thing?"

153

"That's what Terry and I were arguing about the first time you came here. Terry knew I'd been to Bill's that Sunday night, because he was watching."

"Is he usually so obsessive?"

Sybil said, "He says he loves me." The words hung awkwardly in the air. To destroy them, she switched on the television.

"Recapping today's main stories," said the announcer, "the Leader of the Opposition claims the Government's tax package is a confidence trick played on voters; the Australian cricket team is soundly beaten by England; Inspector Carol Ashton hints at an early arrest in the Black and Decker murder case."

"Carol, is that true?"

"I said that to put the pressure on, but we're getting closer."

"To whom?"

"I can't discuss that."

Sybil felt uncertainty after uncertainty gathering in a huge wave that would soon break over her. "Can't you tell me anything?"

"Only that I'm a little concerned about your safety."

Startled, Sybil said, "My safety? But why? Has something else happened?"

"It's just that your name keeps coming up — I can't give you any details — but it makes me feel uneasy."

Sybil couldn't keep the sarcasm out of her voice: "Oh? Does this mean I'm not a suspect any more, but a potential victim?"

"Let's just say I'd feel better if you'd agree to have an officer with you in the house."

Sybil shook her head. "No."

"How about outside, sitting inconspicuously in a car?"

"No."

Carol smiled faintly. "Thought that's what you'd say. Will you at least promise me to be extra careful? Try to avoid being alone with any one person, if you can help it?"

"Can I make you the exception?"

Carol's eyes met hers. "Isn't this the program you want to watch?" she said in her cool silver voice.

"After this message from our sponsor," Pierre Brand was saying, "We'll bring you the latest in one of the most sensational murder cases of the decade, the so-called Black and Decker murder. The victim? The son of the ex-Premier of New South Wales, Sir Richard Pagett, who is battling accusations of corruption during his term of office. Vital questions about his slain son remain unanswered — who drilled a hole in Bill Pagett's head? A slighted lover? A jealous husband? One of the students at Bellwhether High where Bill was a popular industrial arts teacher? And then, there's the death of his best friend, Tony Quade, in a mysterious fall from a cliff. All this, and more, after this important message. . . ."

"What I can't really face," said Sybil, "is that there's someone out there who hates me, enough to set me up for murder. But why? What have I done?"

"You may not have done anything. Besides, the person's motives could seem quite unreasonable to anyone normal."

"It is someone at school, someone I know?"

Carol nodded soberly. "Almost certainly."

"Couldn't it be someone else? Someone who's quite insane? A maniac of some sort?"

"You're looking for a way out, Sybil. You want it to be some fruitcake who pops out of the woodwork for a little murder or two, and then conveniently disappears. It won't work. It's someone connected with Bellwhether High."

They were interrupted by the reappearance of Pierre Brand, his face set in serious lines. "We bring you this story in the interests of justice," he began.

"And ratings," added Carol sarcastically.

There followed a laudatory outline of Bill Pagett's life, with shots of Sir Richard, grieving family members, short interviews with friends, relations and acquaintances, including the brief appearance of Edwina and Lynne together. "That was the kind of man Bill Pagett was," intoned Pierre Brand. "Who could, who would, kill him in the prime of his life?" The murder itself was covered by a fast selection of different shots, including the body being carried out to a waiting ambulance and a tasteless close-up of a running power drill with Brand's voice-over asking, "What hand held this common tool, found in all workshops, and used it to mercilessly end a life?"

"Abysmal would be too flattering a description for this show," Carol remarked as a commercial break again interrupted. She turned to Sybil. "Did you know Pete McIvor owed Bill Pagett money?"

"Yes."

"Why didn't you tell me? Are there any other little details you've forgotten, Sybil?"

Sybil ignored the comment, saying: "I know about Pete because he asked me for money. He was desperate, he said, because Bill was demanding the five thousand back, and he didn't have it. I got the impression Bill had threatened him about it."

"And you didn't think this was important enough to mention before?"

Sybil thought of Pete's fresh, immature face. "Carol, Pete couldn't kill anyone, and besides, a couple of days after I told him I couldn't lend him more than two thousand, he said it was okay, that someone else had come up with the money."

"You were going to give him two thousand dollars?"

"I knew I'd get it back. Why?"

"It just throws a different light on your relationship with him."

Sybil felt indignant. "Carol, are you suspicious of everything everyone does?"

"That's my job. Do you happen to know who was supplying the five thousand?"

"No." Then she said abruptly, "Is it true you have a son?"

Carol's expression didn't change. "Yes. David. He's nine."

"Do you see him often?"

"Oh, yes. My ex-husband's very correct. He's married again, of course. A nice woman, actually — I like her. I try to see David once a week and sometimes he spends part of his school holidays with me. He's a great kid."

Carol looked at her, coolly waiting for the next question. Damn you! thought Sybil, I won't ask you anything else, not until you want to tell me.

Pierre Brand reappeared, rich with measured enthusiasm. "And now, an exclusive interview with Inspector Carol Ashton, the beautiful blonde police officer with the enviable record of arrests. But even she seems baffled by this intriguing case." Sybil watched, fascinated, as Carol fielded the questions with calm professionalism. The planes of her face were made for television. "You look absolutely stunning," she said to Carol.

Carol gave her a quick smile. "Nothing to do with me," she said, "it's just what I inherited."

With a shock, Sybil saw the screen had switched to her. Pierre Brand's voice continued a commentary as she was shown walking in the car park, turning her face from the cameras at the funeral as Terry took her arm to lead her into the chapel, full face in the funeral director's car when she hadn't realized she was in a viewfinder, with Terry leaning over her speaking confidentially. Pierre Brand was saying, "An intimate friend, Terry Clarke, has been at Sybil Quade's side since Bill Pagett's tragic murder and since the mysterious death of her husband. She knew them both. Has Terry Clarke a reason to be alarmed?"

"God!" exclaimed Sybil, "what's that supposed to mean?"

Carol said drily, "Could be anything from indirectly accusing you of murder to implying you're the Angel of Death bringing destruction to all you know."

Pierre Brand was still talking: "Sybil Quade — an attractive woman who could hold the key to the mystery. What is she really like?" With apprehension Sybil saw the footage that must have been shot that afternoon. The voice continued inexorably. "I went to see her this afternoon . . . here's what I found. . . ."

She saw herself open the door and stand, unwelcoming. Brand had apparently used a hidden microphone, as their voices were quite clear. Her comment about the intrusion of the media at the funeral had been edited out. She watched herself look over his shoulder and say, "You're filming this." To his next comment the screen Sybil exclaimed, "I'd like to push you down the steps!"

The door slammed, and Pierre Brand turned regretfully to the camera and said, "This story is about passion — passion and murder. Sybil Quade is a passionate woman. You have seen that for yourself."

Carol seemed quite unsurprised when Sybil said, "It's been edited!" As she snapped off the set she added, "I don't know why I was stupid enough to threaten to push him down the steps."

"It could be worse," said Carol. "You could have actually picked him up and thrown him."

Sybil was grinning at the picture that made as the phone rang. It was Terry. How could Sybil have been so stupid as to threaten a man like Pierre Brand? She obviously needed comfort and guidance. Terry would be around in a few minutes. "Terry, I won't see you. Don't bother coming round here — I won't open the door. Please leave me alone. I'm not going to argue with you. I mean it, Terry, no." She slammed down the phone.

"Hell!" Her eyes met Carol's. "Don't say it, Carol. I know it's my fault. Terry has that endearing male belief that once you sleep with him you've signed over a good part of your life, and that gives him the authority to make demands and expect them to be met."

"Did you enjoy it?"

Sybil didn't bother to play dumb. "No," she said.

Carol's eyes dropped. "This is an impossible situation," she said.

Sybil felt an unexpected rush of tenderness. "No, it isn't," she said involuntarily, "it can't be. It feels too good. It's got to be possible."

"I should go. You've got to get an early start."

As Carol stood, Sybil thought, what's the use of talking? The words just drive us further and further apart. She went to stand behind Carol, putting her arms around her waist and nuzzling the side of her neck. "Don't leave. I want to cuddle you."

As they slid into an embrace, Carol said, "It's so easy to give in to you."

159

They made love wordlessly, with an aching tenderness that was almost frightening to Sybil. Afterwards, with her mouth against Carol's bare shoulder, tasting the salt, she said, "Are you happy?"

"Just at this moment, I'm content."

"That's not enough."

Carol moved restlessly. "It's the best I can offer."

Chapter Eleven

"I've got a report on the anonymous letter," said Bourke.

Carol was preoccupied. She dumped her briefcase on the desk. "Yes? In summary, what does it say?"

"The person who wrote it is obviously well-educated. The printing is, of course, disguised. The pen is a common ballpoint, identical to the government issue pens given to teachers. The paper and envelope are mass produced and can be bought from any one of a thousand news agents or shops. Of the smudged fingerprints on the envelope, the only identifiable ones belong to Mrs. Farrell and Florrie Dunstane and on the letter itself, only Mrs. Farrell's."

"How did it check out with samples of handwriting?"

Bourke made a face. "Inconclusive. The expert wasn't willing to pick anyone out as a definite possibility. He did say it was unlikely to be Evan Berry or Hilary Cosgrove."

"Did you manage to contact Pete McIvor and Terry Clarke?"

"McIvor's waiting outside. Clarke's on his way."

Pete McIvor was like a puppy, anxious to please, but unwilling to admit he had done anything wrong. Carol's patience began to erode. "So this argument between Bill Pagett and Terry Clarke just slipped your mind?"

"Well, not exactly."

Carol leaned forward. "Mr. McIvor," she said, "this is a murder case. Two people have been killed. When you were first interviewed you played dumb, didn't you?"

Pete was flushed and confused. "I didn't think it was important."

Carol raised her eyebrows. "Oh? Not important that Bill Pagett was threatened by Terry Clarke just the day before he was murdered? Come now, Mr. McIvor, what *would* you regard as important?"

"Terry wouldn't have done that to Bill. He might have beaten him up, but a drill. . . ."

"You're an expert on criminal psychology, Mr. McIvor?"

Pete grew even redder at her sarcasm. "No, of course not. But Terry often said things to Bill . . . I mean, they didn't get on. . . ."

"Let me see if I understand you: not only did Clarke threaten Bill Pagett on the beach the Sunday before he died, but this was just one of a series of disagreements the two had had over some time."

162

Pete shifted uncomfortably. "When you put it like that, it sounds bad."

"It does, Mr. McIvor. Perhaps now you'll be willing to be frank."

Skewered by Carol's cold green eyes, Pete McIvor capitulated. "All right, this is what happened that Sunday morning. I'd been surfing, and when I came out of the water I ran into Bill. He wanted to talk to me about something."

"The five thousand you owed him?" Bourke said.

Pete looked, if possible, even more miserable. "Yes. I said I was getting the money on Monday, and he said all right. Then Terry Clarke came up. He ignored me and started shoving Bill in the chest, telling him to leave Syb alone. Bill said Syb didn't want to be left alone, and Terry started swearing. I was sure he was going to hit Bill, but Bill didn't seem worried. In fact, he laughed at Terry, and told him he had a date with Syb that evening and she was going to stay the whole night with him."

"And then what?"

"Terry looked as if he was going to punch Bill, but then he thought better of it. He told Bill he was sure Syb wouldn't waste her time on him, and started to walk off. Bill called out after him, and I thought he'd come back, but he didn't."

"What did he call out?"

Pete looked unhappy. "The exact words?"

"The exact words."

"He said something like, 'Syb's a randy little bitch, but you wouldn't know that, would you — you've never rammed it up her like I have.'"

Carol played with a pen. "What did you take that to mean?" she said after a pause.

163

"Why, that Syb had made love with Bill, but not with Terry."

"Do you know if there was any truth in that?"

Pete shook his head. "Syb's my friend, but I don't have anything to do with her private life."

Bourke said, "And what was the reason you had for keeping quiet about this?"

Pete groaned. "Ah, jeez, it was Terry. He got me on Monday, after we'd heard about Bill, and he said he'd shut up about the five thousand I owed Bill if I shut up about his argument on the beach."

"But you said you had the five thousand to pay back."

"Well, yes, I thought I had, but it fell through. It was going to be from my mum, actually, but when my dad found out it was for gambling debts, he wouldn't let her give me the money."

"And you realized that gave you some sort of motive for the murder."

"I wouldn't have killed anyone for five thousand."

Carol smiled sarcastically. "But you have your price, do you?"

"No, of course not. I just thought it would be easier all round if the whole thing was forgotten."

Carol leaned back and glanced at Bourke. He flipped over a page and said, "Mr. McIvor, you've had a lot of days absent from school, and the term is only a few weeks old."

"I was sick." He sighed. "Well, actually I took some time off to try and get the five thousand. It mightn't sound like much money, but Bill was turning nasty about it."

"This is just one of a series of gambling debts you've struggled to pay over the last year or so, isn't it?"

He looked sulky. "I've had a run of bad luck, that's all."

164

"Three weeks ago, on a Wednesday, you were absent from school."

"Was I? I don't remember."

"Who took your sports duty that afternoon?"

"I don't know. A relief teacher, maybe. I never asked."

A constable put his head around the door. "Inspector? Sorry to interrupt, but there's a Mr. Clarke to see you."

Carol nodded. "Give me two or three minutes, then bring him in." To Pete she said, "Please go with Detective Bourke to make a formal statement." She watched him anxiously groom his mustache as he left. Stupid fool, she thought, why the hell would Sybil offer to give you two thousand dollars?

Her eyes narrowed as Terry Clarke was ushered into the room. He sat down without a word and stared flatly at her. "Well?" he said at last.

"Pete McIvor has told us you had an argument with Bill Pagett on Bellwhether Beach the Sunday morning before he died."

"Has he? Did he tell you Bill was leaning on him about money he owed?"

"Yes, he did."

"And that Bill said unless he got the money on Monday, he'd arrange for someone to come and break Pete's legs?"

"What I'm interested in," said Carol, "is *your* argument with Bill Pagett."

Terry looked impatient. "Look, I told the bastard to leave Syb alone. He was a nasty piece of work, you know. Said things about her that made me want to shove his teeth back down his throat. But I wouldn't kill him. I've told you, he wasn't worthwhile killing."

"You agreed with Pete McIvor to keep the whole scene on the beach quiet, didn't you?"

165

Terry gave her a black frown. "Of course I did. Why go looking for trouble?"

Carol stared at her fingers as she played with a pen. "Did you follow Sybil Quade when she went to Pagett's place on Sunday night?"

"Did Syb tell you I did?"

"Does it matter?"

Terry leaned back, satisfied. "Syb wouldn't. I can trust her. Suppose the kid, Hilary Cosgrove, told you about Syb being there."

"How do you know about Hilary Cosgrove?"

Terry was darkly amused. "I was sitting in my car, watching to see that Syb was all right. I saw this kid sneaking up the drive. I taught her last year, so I knew who she was — anyway, it was common gossip that Bill had cracked on to her."

Carol hid her distaste, saying mildly, "So you saw Sybil Quade leave?"

"Her car nearly flattened the kid, screaming down Pagett's drive. I followed her home to make sure she made it okay."

Carol raised her eyebrows. "Do you often secretly follow her around?"

"I'm keeping an eye on her."

"I'm sure she appreciates that."

Terry stood up. "Don't get smart with me," he said.

Carol looked at him reflectively. "Were you watching her the night Tony Quade died? Perhaps she had an appointment with her husband on Bellwhether Headland and you saw them meet."

"I don't know anything about Quade's death, and neither does Syb. Can I go now?"

At the door, he turned back to say, "You can't pin anything on Syb, so don't try. Why don't you ask Pete if

166

he wanted his legs broken, eh? Seems to me he had a perfect reason to want Pagett dead."

"But why would Pete McIvor want to kill Tony Quade?"

Terry grinned wolfishly. "Maybe you're not so smart, lady cop. What if Quade died accidentally? Or took a dive himself? You just want to make a bigger splash on television — I see you every night on the box. You love it, don't you — all the attention?"

Carol smiled at him. "You'll be asking for my autograph next," she said.

* * * * *

Carol drove to a car park overlooking the beach. She sat in her car, gazing at the waves rolling to the beige sand, the surfers riding, falling, heads bobbing in the white breaking water, and thought of Sybil.

Thought of how many people she had seen involved in violence, and of the heightened emotions, the intensity, the sharp-edged brilliance of life contrasted to death.

You won't feel this way, Sybil, when your world stabilizes, when normality returns, when I no longer have power over you.

Give it up now, she said to herself. Don't drag it out. Don't let yourself be seduced by passion, by promises, by love. She shut her eyes. Come on, don't feel sorry for yourself. You've already gone too far. Get out now.

* * * * *

Edwina looked up, surprised, as Carol opened the front gate. "Doing some gardening," she said, brushing

167

ineffectually at the dirt clinging to the knees of her floral overalls.

"I wonder if you'd mind discussing a few things with me."

Edwina was delighted with her words. "Discussing!" she said cheerfully. "What happened to interrogations? Where are the bright lights and rubber hoses?"

Carol smiled moderately. "Could we talk?" she said.

Edwina led the way through to the veranda at the back of the house. Carol, looking with admiration at the view of water and yachts, said, "I believe your mother lives with you."

Edwina gave a snort of laughter. "She's an invalid. In the front room. Do you want to see her to make sure I'm not making her up? After all, this could be *Psycho,* and I could be a Norman Bates."

Carol had a vision of Anthony Perkins, thin and gangling, standing beside Edwina's rather fuller form. "May I say hello to her?"

Carol wanted to see for herself how alert Mrs. Carter was. Bourke had noted that Edwina had used her mother as an alibi the night Tony Quade had died, adding in pencil on his report, 'might be a bit ga-ga, and confused about the day and time.'

She found a charming little woman sitting up in bed, vague but polite, who confused Carol with an old friend's daughter and began a rambling story that Edwina finally cut off with, "Time for your sleep, Mum."

Carol didn't comment on Mrs. Carter as they returned to the beautiful view. Instead she said, "You helped Mrs. Quade with baseball a week or so ago, didn't you?"

Edwina shrugged. "I'm the bunny who's expected to fill in when anyone's away on a sport afternoon. Why? What's it got to do with anything?"

"Did you return all the bats to the sports store?"

Edwina laughed. "You kidding? The PE Department are so slack they don't know what equipment they've got, let alone what they should have. Anyway, Syb took the stuff back. Why don't you ask her?"

Carol ignored that, saying, "You've been on television a couple of times."

Edwina gestured for her to sit down. "Are we going to be discussing my budding television career?"

"Not exactly. What I am interested in is the information being supplied to Pierre Brand."

Edwina pouted. "You'll have to ask Lynne about that. It's nothing to do with me."

"But it is. Mr. Brand wasn't very cooperative, but he did eventually admit that you have been supplying him with inside information. For example, he mentioned that you have given him information about anonymous letters received by Mrs. Farrell."

Edwina was unrepentant. "So? It's a free country. I can say what I like."

"How did you know about the letters to Mrs. Farrell?"

Edwina was scornful. "You can't be a very good detective if you don't know that already. Florrie told me."

"We've already spoken to Mrs. Dunstane. I wondered if you'd tell the truth."

Edwina beamed at her. "I always tell the truth if I think a lie will be found out."

"How did Pierre Brand know Mrs. Quade had gone home early yesterday afternoon?"

"I rang him and told him."

"Do you get paid for these little tips?" asked Carol.

"Of course. You don't think I'd do it for love?"

"How about hate?"

169

Edwina's face was flushed and there was a line of perspiration along her upper lip. "Hate Syb? Why should I hate her?"

"Do you know several people have received anonymous telephone calls like the one you had?"

"Yes, of course I do. Lynne went on and on about hers and how she felt and how Bruce had to keep the kids because she thought they were in danger." She set her mouth. "Stupid bitch," she added. She looked over at Carol. "And, Inspector, Alan and Syb had calls. Have I missed anyone? Don't tell me Phyllis Farrell! I can just see her face."

"Did you tell anyone that you had received a call?"

Edwina's face became mottled. She heaved herself to her feet. "I told you, Inspector, because it's your job to know. But why the hell do you think I'd go round telling anyone else someone called me a bag of lard and threatened to push me off a cliff?"

Carol nodded. "Okay. Thanks for your help."

* * * * *

Sunday was gray and heavy. Carol groaned as Bourke dumped a bulging folder in front of her. "Why can't it be like the movies?" she complained. "They never get all this paperwork."

Bourke's enthusiasm was not infectious. Carol hadn't slept well and her head was aching, but she was determined to plow through the work with Bourke to get it out of the way. She thought of Sybil and wondered what she was doing.

"Sybil Quade," said Bourke. "Did I startle you, Carol?"

"I was just thinking. What about her?"

"Did you see her lose her temper with Brand on his program? I told you she was passionate. And why has she been so reluctant to tell us the truth? I mean, everything we know has been dragged out of her, bit by bit. Do you think she's protecting someone?"

In her imagination Carol could see the turn of her head and her quick smile. "Who?" she said.

"How about Terry Clarke? I can't believe they're not sleeping together. I mean, who could resist Terry? He has a kind of neanderthal charm, don't you think?"

"Are you trying to be funny?" said Carol.

Bourke grinned. "Not if it doesn't please you, Carol, and it obviously doesn't. About Sybil, though — could she be scared of Terry? Intimidated into keeping quiet? He is pretty formidable."

"I don't think so."

"Okay, then, let's look at Pete McIvor. After all, she was willing to give him two thousand dollars with no likelihood of getting it back. So how about Pete and Sybil as lovers? I'm sure she could get him to do anything she liked."

"You mean murder someone for her?"

"Well, it's a popular motive, and, like I said, even I might kill for her." He smiled at Carol's expression. "I see Pete doesn't meet with your favor, either. Well, there's always Alan Witcombe."

"You see Sybil Quade having an affair with Alan Witcombe?"

"I admit it does require an imaginative leap, but you know as well as I do it's not impossible. All that concentration on sex and sin isn't much good without a healthy outlet — and you don't get much healthier than our Syb. Remember, Alan told me he thinks Sybil's absolutely wonderful."

171

"I find your flippancy this morning quite wearing," said Carol, opening the folder. "How are your inquiries about nail polish going?"

"Oh, fair go!" said Bourke. "It's uphill work. You won't be surprised to learn that nail polish color isn't a vivid memory in most people's minds."

"Does Edwina Carter wear nail polish?"

Bourke sighed. "Frequently. And so does every second female on the staff at least some of the time."

"Sybil Quade? I haven't seen her wearing it."

"Maybe she's given it up, since the murder."

"All right, Mark, keep at it."

"Okay," said Bourke, "but you know if it's a woman, she almost certainly changed the color of her nails right after the murder."

"Yes," said Carol, "that's what we're looking for."

* * * * *

When Sir Richard rang, Bourke had gone and Carol was staring moodily at a glass of whiskey. "Yes, Sir Richard, Mark Bourke and I have just finished reviewing the evidence to date."

Sir Richard had seen Pierre Brand's program on Friday night. He was interested in Sybil Quade's angry threat to push Brand down the steps. Had Carol spoken to her? As Brand had pointed out, she was a passionate woman.

As Carol assured Sir Richard she had interviewed Mrs. Quade on several occasions, she thought of Sybil's naked skin, the smooth line of her back, the way her body arched as she climaxed. "Mrs. Quade may have been responding to the pressure exerted by the media — she's a very private person," she said.

172

"Has she admitted she had an affair with my son?"

"No."

Sir Richard was impatient. "Well, get it out of her. Bill gave me to understand they were lovers."

"At the same time as he was going with Hilary Cosgrove?"

"Well, Inspector, that gives a perfect motive. Sybil Quade is in love with Bill, but he throws her over for someone younger and more attractive."

Carol couldn't resist. "Have you met Mrs. Quade?" she said.

"Not in the flesh. No."

"If you had, you wouldn't imagine she'd be passed over for someone else."

"Oh?" said Sir Richard. "But isn't that exactly what happened? Her husband dumped her, didn't he?"

* * * * *

Mrs. Farrell's hand hesitated over the phone, then she lifted it, checked a number and dialed. "Inspector Ashton? Sorry to worry you at home on a Sunday, but there's one little detail about the day Mr. Pagett died that's been bothering me. I know it may sound rather ridiculous, but it's about clashing colors."

Chapter Twelve

For Sybil, Monday mornings at school after a perfect summer weekend always had a certain depression about them, and this one was par for the course. The two days spent in the peaceful calm of Barbara's friendship receded like a dream as she walked in to hear Terry exclaiming, "Jesus! It's the bloody swimming carnival tomorrow! If there's one thing I hate, it's wet, screaming kids."

"You don't seem very keen on dry, screaming kids, either," observed Edwina, who, extraordinarily, was knitting.

"Getting ready for winter?" said Sybil, looking at the red wool. She bent over as Edwina gave a confidential nod.

"Diet," said Edwina softly. "Got to do something with my hands, or I eat."

"Good luck."

"I'll need it."

"What are you two whispering about?" said Lynne.

"You," said Edwina. "That should make you happy."

Lynne's vitriolic retort was prevented by Alan's entry with the schedule of duties for the next day's swimming carnival. "Now look," he said to the murmurs of protest, "it's only once a year and it's for the good of the school. I know it can be inconvenient, but we just all pull our weight and it will be a great success."

"You have clichés for breakfast?" inquired Edwina.

Alan ignored that. "And it's very fair. The Physical Education Department drew lots to determine which teachers had to travel to the Warringah Swimming Center on a bus."

"I'll bet not one of the PE staff got bus duty," said Pete, reading the list. He grunted. "Well, Lynne, you and I are awfully lucky. We get a whole bus of kids each."

"Let me see that!" Lynne looked furious. "I particularly told them I didn't want bus duty. I have to get the catering for lunches done. If you want to eat, one of you had better do my duty for me."

"I'll do it," said Sybil.

Alan shook his head. "No you won't," he said. "I've arranged with Mrs. Farrell for you to take the day off. She agrees you've been under a tremendous amount of strain in the past couple of weeks, and it's a perfect opportunity to let you have an extra break."

"Wonderful!" said Lynne. "*I'm* feeling the strain, too. Do I get some time off?"

"Oh, don't be so selfish, Lynne," said Pete in an unexpected attack. She glared at him as he continued, "Syb's had a much worse time than any of us, so leave her alone. And you can stop bitching about bus duty. I'll find someone to do it for you."

Terry drew Sybil aside. "I've got a Shooting Association meeting tonight. I can't get to your place till late, probably after eleven."

"Terry, I'm tired after the weekend. Let's leave it until tomorrow."

"Okay," he said reluctantly. He took her by the elbows, "And Syb, I want to talk about moving in with you."

Sybil looked at his opaque dark eyes. I could beat you over the head with a club, she thought, and I'd still never get through to you. "I'm willing to talk about it, if you insist, but it's impossible."

"Why? There isn't anyone else."

"There is."

She felt wryly amused at his astonishment.

* * * * *

As soon as she had a break, Sybil rang Carol, using the phone in Alan's office so she wouldn't be overheard. Although Carol sounded reserved, she said quite readily, "Yes, I'll come and see you. What time?"

"If I leave straight after the last lesson, I'll be home by four at the latest. Could you meet me then?"

Carol's voice was faintly amused. "You're keen," she said.

176

"Yes." Sybil let the silence stretch for a moment, then said, "Could you park in the Singleton's place, behind me, and come in the back way? They're away for a week, so you can park in their carport. The reporters were waiting in the street for me when I left this morning, and I'm sure you don't want to see them any more than I do." Suddenly she felt prickly and dissatisfied. "Carol, are you sure you want to come?"

"I'll see you about four," said Carol.

* * * * *

Bourke rubbed his sweaty hands with a handkerchief and glared at the ancient fan, whose whirling blades created an extraordinary humming clatter as they stirred the heavy hot air. "Why don't they air-condition suburban police stations?" When Carol raised an eyebrow at his irritation, he sighed and said, "This is driving me mad. You know, it's bloody impossible to keep track of every kid who ran a message for a teacher the day Pagett died. And it's such a long shot, Carol."

"You said any pupil leaving the school grounds has to have a permission slip from a teacher."

Bourke nodded. "Yes, and senior students on the gates collect them at recess and lunchtime. I've got two officers interviewing the seniors, but the kid could have been sent out during class time."

"Then the important thing would be whose class the student came from, wouldn't it?"

Bourke made a face at Carol. "So what if we find out? It's not enough to prove anything for sure."

"Another brick in the wall," said Carol, "and every brick counts."

* * * * *

Sybil was home before four. She felt restless and unsettled — she ached to see Carol, but dreaded what she might say. She stood just inside the glass doors waiting for her, and when Carol drew up her skin prickled with excitement and fear. She watched Carol unhurriedly climb out of her car, stand as if deciding what to do, then turn towards the house.

Sybil opened the door before Carol could knock. "I thought for a moment you weren't going to come in," she said. Why can't I play hard to get? she thought. Before Carol could reply she continued hastily, "Let me get you a pair of shorts and a top. We can go for a walk, or a swim, if you like."

Carol's voice was cool. "No. Reporters might be a problem."

"Carol, is something wrong?"

"It's just that I'm tired, and. . . ."

Sybil met the direct green eyes, thinking, this is when she says goodbye Sybil — been nice to know you. "And what?"

"And the last thing I need in my life at the moment is you as a complication. Sybil, do you understand?"

Ignore it, thought Sybil, and the words will go away. "You're the only person who calls me Sybil, everyone else calls me Syb."

Carol gave her a faint smile. "That must be a thrill for you," she observed, opening her briefcase. She handed Sybil an envelope and a letter, both in a protective plastic sheath. "Ever seen anything like these before?"

"Yes, somewhere."

"Where?"

178

"I don't know — in one of those leather writing cases — do you know the sort I mean?"

"Yes. What color was it?"

"It was red leather, I think. I'm sorry, I can't remember where I saw it."

"Who did it belong to? A woman?"

"Possibly. I just have a sort of mental picture of the red leather, square white envelopes and sheets of heavy writing paper."

"It's not unusual stationery," said Carol.

"No, but you asked me if I'd seen anything like it, and I have. I can't remember where, though."

"Read it," said Carol.

It was the last letter Mrs. Farrell had received. Carol watched Sybil's eyes traversing the lines, stopping and rereading. With an expression of distaste she handed it back. "Who wrote it?"

"We don't know. Do you recognize the printing?"

"No, but of course it's disguised, isn't it?"

Carol nodded. "Yes. Probably done left-handed." She glanced at Sybil's fingers. "Or, in your case, right-handed."

"You don't think I wrote it? Carol, you can't!"

"I don't think you wrote it. It's almost certain the murderer's responsible. That's just one of a series Mrs. Farrell has been receiving for months. All the others were on the subject of Bill Pagett and his sexual activities." She put the letter and envelope back into her briefcase. "You were mentioned several times," she added.

"Why me?"

"That's the important question, isn't it?"

What in the hell do I say to that? thought Sybil. Aloud she said, "Can't we get out of here? Drive somewhere and then walk?"

179

"Okay, lend me something to change into. We'd better use my car — your numberplate is far too well known, now."

As they walked to the gate in the back fence leading to the Singleton's house, Carol said, "Where's Terry?"

"I'm seeing him tomorrow. He's got a meeting tonight, and I told him I was going to bed early." She looked sideways at Carol. She hadn't meant it that way, but it sounded like an invitation. She was alive with irritated energy. "Can I drive?" she asked as they reached the car.

Carol handed her the keys and settled into the passenger seat, saying, "Where are we going?"

"West Head. Is that okay?"

"Why not?"

The traffic was reasonably heavy until they took the turning at McCarr's Creek into Ku-ring-gai National Park. She stopped to pay the ranger at the entrance, then settled down to the smooth uninterrupted drive along the bushland peninsula. The road dipped and curved through the grey-green vegetation, slabs of rock glistened with seeping water, birds soared in the updrafts and the shadows of clouds chased themselves over gum trees and native bushes. Every now and then they caught a glimpse of a vivid blue sliver of water. Sybil finally broke the silence. "Why did you get divorced?"

Carol let her breath out in a long sigh. "I don't particularly want to talk about it."

"Oh great!" said Sybil. "Your whole career is making people answer questions, but you get a bit shy when you're in the hot seat."

"All right, Sybil."

"Carol, I'm only asking because it's important for me to know."

Carol made no further comment, but told the story with unemotional economy as though she wanted to get the task over and done with. She had met Justin Hart while studying at Sydney University, and, attracted by his formidable mind and legal talent, had married him. In due course she produced a son, David. Because they both had demanding and time-consuming careers, they lived, in the main, separate lives. Perhaps they would have continued reasonably happily, had Carol not fallen in love with a woman. "I knew at some level that I was attracted to women, but it wasn't a problem until I met Christine. I loved her so much I was willing to put everything on the line for her, and in the end, that's what I lost — everything."

Carol and Justin had agreed there was nothing left in their marriage, so they should divorce. Carol hoped to keep custody of David, or at least share him, but she found she couldn't fight the wealth, influence, and arguments of her husband — wasn't it best for a child to have a normal background? When he was older would David be happy to find he had a deviate for a mother? Was Carol intending to live with Christine? How would David explain the situation to his friends?

"Now, I would have fought him, openly. Then . . . I was younger, Christine had begged me not to make a scandal — in short, I was persuaded to give David up. And, of course, I've regretted it."

They had reached the spectacular lookout at the end of West Head. Sybil parked the car and twisted around to look at Carol's face. "Christine?"

"She's fine. I see her photo sometimes in the social pages, and she always sends me a Christmas card."

"So it was all for nothing?"

Carol opened the car door. "Nothing?" she said, smiling sardonically. "I learned a great deal about love, life and constancy. Come on, if you want to have a walk, let's walk."

* * * * *

It had been an extraordinarily tense afternoon, with both of them avoiding the subject of their relationship. They had walked, gazed at the beautiful view over Lion Island and Broken Bay, watched the yachts tacking against the breeze and, in unspoken agreement, talked about safe things — music, films, books. Now that they were back inside Sybil's house, the physical longing that had dogged Sybil all weekend suddenly became too much to bear.

"Carol. . . ."

"I don't want to do this."

Sybil pushed her gently back against the wall, put a hand on either side of her head, and began to kiss her — slowly, deeply, feeling her excitement rise as Carol began to respond.

Carol turned her head away. "Remember, you think this is unnatural."

Sybil, slipping her hands under Carol's shirt to circle her back, said, "I've changed my mind." Her tongue found the hollow of Carol's throat. I wish there were some way I could say I love you without sounding like an adolescent fool, she thought. Aloud she said, "Come to bed."

"Sybil, this is stupid and dangerous."

Sybil slid her fingers up under Carol's bra and caressed a nipple. "Don't you want this?" she said against Carol's mouth.

182

"Yes, I want it now . . . it's afterwards."

Carol caught her breath as Sybil began to unzip her denim shorts. She put her hands over Sybil's. "Afterwards, it isn't worth it," she said.

Sybil pulled her hands away and began to push the shorts down. Carol groaned as Sybil's fingers slid between her legs.

"It's not fair," she gasped, "you've found my weak point."

Sybil knelt, and began to melt her with the soft, insistent pressure of her tongue.

"Oh, darling," Carol said as her orgasm began.

*   *   *   *   *

Sybil was content. Carol was curled around her, the moonlight made patterns of light and dark on the bed, her body floated in the delicious relaxation that followed passion. She turned in Carol's arms to face her. "What are you thinking about?" she said.

The planes of Carol's face were sculptured by moonlight but her eyes were shadowed. "I don't think you want to know."

"Tell me."

Carol released her, turning on her back and gazing up at the ceiling. "I was thinking how I keep on saying we must never do this again, and then I do."

"*We* do, Carol. It isn't just your decision."

"Sybil, it isn't going to work."

"It will if we want it to."

"You haven't thought of the difficulties."

"Carol, of course I have. I'm not a fool. I know there'll be problems, but so what? It will be worth it."

183

Carol turned, leaning on one elbow to look down at her. "You can't live at this intensity of emotion for very long."

"I don't expect to. There'll be more than this — friendship, companionship — someone always there."

Carol sat up, resting her chin on her knees. Her silver voice was calmly reasonable. "Sybil, my job means I see people in crisis situations. I know what happens. You met me when you were vulnerable. Now you've had your first lesbian relationship. You might go on to have others, you might return to the conventional straight world —"

Sybil interrupted. "I won't go back, not now."

"Whatever you do, you have to remember that all this, you and I, happened because your safe world was destroyed and you were frightened and insecure."

Sybil sat up in turn. "You took advantage of me, did you?"

"In a way, I did."

"How unethical!" said Sybil mockingly.

Carol swung her legs off the bed. "I'm going," she said.

Sybil was suddenly furious. "Running away, are you Carol? You can't stand to be responsible for your own, or anyone else's emotions, can you? While I was rejecting the feelings we had for each other, that was fine, wasn't it? You were safe. Now, when I want to accept our relationship, to love you — suddenly you're rationalizing everything away."

"I'm not going to argue with you."

"Why not? Afraid I might win?"

Carol began to dress. "Sybil, let's cool it for now? Okay?"

"No, it's not okay."

Carol sighed. "Suit yourself."

"And don't sigh at me!" Sybil wanted to hit her, anything to get something other than the glassy surface of her indifference. She seized her shoulders. "Carol, I've never felt like this before, not with anyone."

"Don't mistake sex for love."

"God! You sound like a nineteen-sixties advice to the lovelorn column." In her rage she shook her. "It's a lot more than sex. Come on, Carol, say you love me. You do. You must."

"What? And join the queue?" She twisted free of Sybil's hands. "You're so infinitely desirable, Sybil . . . Terry Clarke follows you around, Bill Pagett couldn't keep his hands off you, your husband came back from overseas. . . ." She shrugged. "Why not put this down to an interesting experience — your little excursion into lesbianism — a harmless little dabble in forbidden sex?"

"You're deliberately picking a fight, Carol."

"Why would I bother?"

"To make it easier to leave. To make sure the last memories are sour ones."

"Sybil, if things had been different —"

"That's rubbish, and you know it. Why don't you be honest, Carol? Just say it's been nice, but I took it all a bit seriously, and you're sorry if I'm hurt, but that's the way it is. Have I got the dialogue right?"

"Just about," said Carol.

Sybil didn't cry when she had gone, but sat cross-legged in the pool of moonlight on the bed, trying resolutely to construct a world for herself in which there was no Carol.

* * * * *

185

The clock radio woke Sybil at six-thirty. Half awake, she felt the looming grayness of sadness and disappointment, and then, as she opened her eyes, she unwillingly remembered the night before. She looked at the crumpled sheets and tried to imagine Carol's naked body curled around her. "I'm not going to cry," she said to Jeffrey, who was perched on the end of the bed to lobby for breakfast.

At seven-thirty she picked up the phone, and began to dial Carol's number. Before she had finished, she replaced the receiver. She'd be out running, or be at the station, or not want to talk to Sybil anyway. What was there left to say? I love you, Carol? Someone else had said that to Carol before, and she didn't want to hear it again.

The day stretched ahead of her, empty. She went around the house opening all the windows to the summer air. Cicadas shrilled, the air shimmered with early heat, a small flock of cockatoos shrieked and whirled in insolent acrobatics. Standing at the open glass doors, staring at the sea, she could almost believe she would rather be at the swimming carnival, coping with the excited screams of students echoing against the tiles and glass of the indoor pool. She could just turn up and offer to help. Then she thought of Terry. The heavy weight of his obsession would suffocate her. She didn't want to see him today, or ever.

"Come on, Jeffrey, entertain me," she said to his fat purring ginger face.

Chapter Thirteen

"What's the matter?" Bourke said.

"Mark, it's her, I know it." Carol paced the small office. "And she's going to do something else. She's getting such a charge out of this, she isn't going to stop now."

"We haven't got enough, Carol."

"I know that, but it all adds up. Lynne knew about Edwina's threatening call, even though Edwina swears she told no one but us. Lynne was rostered to give out

187

sports equipment, including baseball bats, on the two Wednesdays before Pagett's murder. . . ."

"So she had access to the bats, Carol — that doesn't prove anything."

Carol rubbed her forehead. "All right, but add to that the change of nail color. Lynne was late to school that Monday morning, and Mrs. Farrell watched her sign in. She says she's sure Lynne was wearing pale pink polish on her nails. Yet by the time the staff meeting was called, it had changed to a dark red color — Mrs. Farrell noticed it when Lynne interrupted us both on the way to the meeting. I knew something was nagging me about that first interview we had with Lynne — it was the clash between the dark pink dress she was wearing and that purple red polish. Plus there's the kid you found who ran a message for her to the local shops to get a bottle of nail polish . . . and she specifically said she wanted a *dark* color."

"She'd come up with some reasonable explanation," said Bourke.

"I'm sure she chipped off polish while she was killing Bill Pagett, and knew that she had to do something to hide it. *She* couldn't leave the school without being noticed, so she sent a kid. If we could only match the flakes of nail polish vacuumed up from the workroom floor. . . ."

"She'll have ditched that particular bottle of pink polish."

"Mark, know how you said whoever it was was laughing at us? Well, I'm sure you're right, and now Lynne Simpson believes she's gotten away with murder twice. She makes a move, and we follow — but we don't seem to ever get close to her. She's puffed up with confidence and pride, and that makes her terribly dangerous."

"She wouldn't risk anything now."

"Ring Bellwhether and get me the names of any teachers absent from today's swimming carnival." She paced around as he made the call. "Well?"

"Mrs. Farrell arranged for Sybil Quade to take the day off, so she's away. A couple of other teachers reported in sick, but they're nothing to do with the case. Everyone else we're interested in has gone to the carnival, except Alan Witcombe, who's sitting in the main office right now, entering student grades into a computer."

"The carnival's at Warringah Swimming Center, isn't it? Get them on the phone. I want to be sure Lynne Simpson is there."

* * * * *

Sybil looked at her watch. Only ten-thirty. The morning was dragging by like a professional cripple. The sound of someone at the door was a welcome relief.

"Hello, Syb. Aren't you going to ask me in?"

"I thought you'd be at the swimming carnival," said Sybil, standing aside.

Lynne brushed past her, laden with a huge plastic shopping bag. "Can't leave it in the car," she said, "Got meat and salad things in it." She placed it carefully on the floor and turned to say, "I hope you're not criticizing me for running out on my duty, Syb. After all, you're here at home, not supervising wet, shrieking kids in boring races." She looked appreciatively out at the sea. "Isn't it a stunning day? Makes you glad to be alive."

Lynne was her usual polished self but, rarely for her, was dressed in tailored slacks and a tunic top. She saw

189

Sybil glance at her clothes, and said, "I'm dressed to do my duty, Syb. I endured the smell of chlorine and patter of wet feet for the first few races, and now I've slipped away. I volunteered to run the staff catering for the day, so I've got senior kids trotting around with tea, coffee and biscuits, and I've just ducked out to pick up cold meats and salad things for lunch. Told everyone I didn't have time to get everything yesterday. And now that I've finished my chores so early, thought I'd pop up here and have a cup of coffee with you. The others can hold the fort for the moment."

"I'll get the coffee."

"Let me help you," said Lynne, picking up the shopping bag and following her out to the kitchen.

Lynne's idea of help was to lean elegantly against the refrigerator watching Sybil spoon coffee into the percolator. She slid her gold bangles off her wrists and placed them neatly on the table. "They're annoying me," she said at Sybil's surprised look.

"You've come a long way to do the shopping for lunch," said Sybil, getting mugs out of the cupboard.

Lynne ignored that, saying, "Syb, is that the cupboard door you hit your cheekbone with? It was quite a spectacular bruise. I thought someone must have punched you."

"Lynne, what do you want? You're not just here for a friendly cup of coffee, are you?"

Lynne checked her gold watch. "No, not exactly."

"Then what?"

Lynne's tone was lightly conversational. "Did you sleep with Bill?"

"What?"

"Oh, come on, Syb. It was obvious he was hot for you. Did you give him what he wanted?"

190

"No, Lynne, I didn't. Why are you asking this?"

"To give you a chance to tell the truth." Lynne pursed her lips reflectively. "Bill said he made love to you."

"Bill lied," said Sybil flatly. "What does it matter now?"

"It matters to me."

Sybil looked at her with astonishment. "What do you mean?"

Lynne was pensive. She gazed out the open kitchen door at the choko vine that threatened to overwhelm the fence. "I loved him, you know," she remarked.

"Bill?"

"Yes. Stupid of me, wasn't it?"

Sybil began to feel faintly alarmed. She poured the coffee into the mugs and handed one to Lynne. "You and Bill . . . I never thought. . . ."

Lynne slid gracefully into a chair at the table. "No? He didn't tell you all the details of how we made love? That surprises me. After all, he told me about what you two did together. And what he did with Hilary Cosgrove."

"Lynne, I didn't have any relationship with Bill at all."

"He was obsessed with you. The others. I didn't care much about them, but *you* . . . you were different."

They sat facing each other at the kitchen table. Lynne played with the stack of gold bangles and sighed. "You're really quite beautiful, you know, Syb."

"Thanks," said Sybil drily.

"When Bill showed me that note you wrote him he said you hated and loved him at the same time. Said you were attracted to him because he made you feel something for the first time in your life. Do you think that's true, Syb? I always thought you were frigid, myself."

191

Sybil took a deep breath. "Lynne, I don't want to discuss any of this."

"Do you think Bill deserved to die?"

"No, I don't. Lynne, don't you think you'd better be getting back to the carnival?"

Lynne checked her watch. "I've still got enough time." She sipped her coffee, then said, "You know, I think if you kill someone, you've really taken control of your life."

Sybil began to feel cold. "Lynne —" she began.

Lynne, reaching over to rummage in her bag, interrupted her. "Syb, darling, randy little bitch you are." She laughed. "Deserve to lose your head."

Sybil stared at her. "You made the phone calls."

"Of course I did. And they were so much more fun than the letters. I made them all, and faked one to myself to fool the cops. Actually, Syb, you took it the best. I quite admired the way you kept your cool. But you always do, don't you Syb? Even now."

Sybil's eyes went to Lynne's hands. She had taken something from the shopping bag.

"Yes, Syb. It is a rifle. One of Terry's rifles, actually. Had to saw off most of the barrel to make it easy to conceal, but it'll still hit something at close range quite satisfactorily. Careless of you never to lock your garage, Syb. Made it simple to plant the metal filings and the rest of the barrel during a couple of free periods I had yesterday. I'll leave it to the police to work out why you bothered to cut it at all."

Lynne seemed quite relaxed, but the black eye of the barrel pointed without wavering at Sybil's face. "Don't try and move, Syb. I need powder burns on your skin. Oh, I see from your expression you understand. You always were bright, weren't you?" Lynne leaned back and flipped

192

the telephone receiver off its cradle. "To prevent interruptions," she said cheerfully.

Sybil was clammy with perspiration. She saw Carol's face in her mind. I love you, she thought. Clearing her tightening throat, she said, "Lynne, why are you going to kill me?"

Lynne was delighted with her. "I knew you wouldn't use the old cliché about how I must be mad or try to persuade me to let you go. You've already worked out that would be hopeless, haven't you? Now I've gone this far, I have to finish it. I'm really sorry, Syb. I've always liked you."

"Not enough, it seems."

"Oh, Syb. I'll miss your dry sense of humor." She shrugged. "But, what can I do?"

"At least tell me why."

Lynne checked her watch. "Okay, but I'll have to be brief. I've got to get back. I did all the shopping yesterday, of course, and it's all ready to go, so I only have to appear with the goodies. It's not really an alibi, but it'll do, especially as you've committed suicide, not been murdered."

Sybil really couldn't believe it. She went to stand up, and the barrel followed her. "No, Syb. Live a little bit longer. You'll find every second counts." Sybil stared at the attractive, perfectly made-up face and subsided in her chair.

* * * * *

"Can't you hurry it up, Mark?"

He shook his head. "The pool attendant's gone to find a teacher." The distant receiver had been flung down, and all Bourke could hear was the muted shrieks of students

193

and a disjointed conversation between two loud-voiced people near the phone.

Carol paced up and down. "Mark?"

"It sounds like a riot's going on," he observed. "Oh, hello, this is Detective Bourke," he began, as someone picked up the phone at the other end.

Prickling with anxious impatience, Carol hovered near the desk. Bourke's face was sober as he replaced the receiver. "Sorry that took so long, but no one seems able to find Lynne Simpson, and her car's gone. They think she's left to get food for the staff lunch."

Carol snatched the phone and dialed. "Sybil Quade's number," she said to Bourke's raised eyebrows. She slammed it down. "It's busy."

*****

"You know," said Lynne, "I find I want to share what I've done, Syb. I suppose you realize I got rid of your husband for you? You have to admit he was no loss."

"How did you do it?" asked Sybil, adding silently — Carol help me.

"Tony? He came to me after the argument he had with Bill over you. He stayed with me Sunday night, and on Monday, when he found out what had happened to Bill, he went into shock. I persuaded him to stay out of sight, and he did. But he knew how I felt about Bill, was asking too many questions, getting too difficult, so I decided to get rid of him. I said I'd told you he was back, and that you wanted to meet him up on Bellwhether Headland late at night. I was kind enough to offer to drive him up there — I said you'd have your car and the two of you would go off together. That fed his ego, so he agreed. Had the baseball bat you obligingly handed back to me when I was on duty

194

in the sports store a couple of weeks ago. The one I used on Bill. You know, Syb, I was quite good at sports when I was at school. It was really laughably simple. It's nerve you know, if you've got nerve you can do anything."

She smiled at Sybil's expression. "Oh, come on, Syb. He was a bastard, and you know it. And so full of himself, he never even thought of me as a threat. I hit him across the side of the head as he walked up and down, asking where you were. Perhaps you'll be flattered to know he was so impatient to see you. I didn't want to kill him straight out and then have to drag his body to the cliff, so I waited till he was semi-conscious and then helped him to his feet and steered him towards the edge. I got him to stand there, dazed, then a quick shove sent him over. He didn't even scream. I checked he hadn't fallen on a ledge or anything, then I left." She frowned at Sybil. "Oh, and I went back after the body had been found and planted the baseball bat. It was stupid of me, actually — should have done it right away. Hoped there might be some of your fingerprints on it. Were there?"

"Yes."

"You know, Syb, I'm a bit disappointed at the police. Would have thought their forensic people could have tested the bat properly."

"What do you mean?"

"Well, I used it on Bill, and then on Tony, but no one's even mentioned that the same weapon was used. Slack, isn't it?" Her smile returned. "You know, I planned everything so well — for example, I hit Bill the way a left-hander would."

"You wanted me arrested."

"I did. But Carol Ashton isn't going to arrest you, is she? *I* would, if I were her. Look at the meat on your Black and Decker — thought it was a nice touch, maybe a bit

195

over the top, but quite in character . . . you always like to be prepared, don't you Syb? That's why your suicide is going to be so neat. There won't be a note, of course, but the general impression will be that you were finally unable to cope with the pressure of investigation — Carol Ashton has been hounding you, of course — and your own feelings of guilt."

"That's very creative, Lynne."

"I'll remember you were sarcastic at the end, Syb. I really like you, you know."

Carol? Sybil thought.

* * * * *

"Inspector Ashton's gone to Sybil Quade's place with Constable Richards," said Bourke to the young uniformed officer. "You're coming with me to Warringah Swimming Center . . . I don't care if you've got something else to do — this is urgent!"

* * * * *

Lynne checked her watch again. "Not much time, Syb."

At Sybil's convulsive movement she stood, scraping the chair against the floor. The eye of the barrel was still centered on Sybil's face. "Everyone wants to live," she said conversationally. "So it would be stupid to do anything impulsive." She smiled. "Why, Syb, someone might rescue you yet. Terry, for instance. Pity he's going to miss his opportunity. He's rostered to start races all morning. Rather amusing to think of him with a little starting pistol, when I've got his rifle. Do you think after

196

your suicide he'll ever forgive himself for not noticing you'd taken his gun?"

Sybil sat apparently still, but she was slowly gathering her feet underneath her. There's a chance I can deflect the barrel, she thought, only a chance, but it's better than sitting here and waiting for a bullet.

"I think I'll shoot out one of your eyes," said Lynne, "then you won't be so beautiful, Syb. You know, I had a choice about killing Bill. My first idea was to drill out his eyes, but when it came to the crunch, I just couldn't do it. Besides, I wasn't sure that would kill him. It's so ironic, Syb, that Tony was the one to give me the perfect method. One evening at Bill's place he was telling us about his uncle who gives pathology evidence in murder cases. It was absolutely fascinating. Isn't it funny how you learn useful things, but you don't realize it at the time?"

"Why did you use a drill at all?"

"Oh, Syb! You disappoint me. Industrial Art! Surely you can see analogies between his work and his behavior and an electric drill? I left him arranged in a sort of tableau though I suppose the police are too stupid to understand the symbolism." Her cheerfulness evaporated. "And I don't believe you when you say you didn't make love with Bill. I know you did. He enjoyed telling me those details about the things you used to do with him."

"Lynne, he was only trying to hurt you. None of it was true."

"Well, of course you'd say that, Syb. But when I saw Bill in his workroom on Monday morning at the end of roll call, he told me what you did together on Sunday night, before Tony turned up. He said you were panting for it, Syb. He said you like a bit of slapping around, that it drove you wild. He was very graphic. It made it all such a pleasure. I don't think he even saw the bat coming."

197

Time, thought Sybil, I've got to give Carol time. "Didn't you have a roll call and then a class?"

"It was simple. I always leave the room as soon as I've called the roll — don't see why I should waste my time staring at kids. I was particularly efficient on Monday. Left my Year Seven roll chattering to each other like magpies, collected the baseball bat, and went straight to Bill's workroom. I had Eleven-ES in the library first period. They're a bright class, you know, and I'd given them a research task that would scatter them from one end of the library shelves to the other. Told them on Friday to go straight to the library and start working. I'm often late to class. I knew they'd never notice, and they didn't."

Sybil couldn't believe they were in her sunny kitchen discussing murder in such conversational tones. Lynne leaned forward confidentially. "And you know what, I thought it wouldn't take long, but really, Syb, it was unbelievable. I don't think I was away more than seven or eight minutes at the most, and when I got back, there was my class, happily working. I just circulated, acting as though I'd been there giving advice from the beginning."

"And no one noticed you carrying a baseball bat around?"

"I put it in a roll of cardboard I took from Edwina's desk. There's nothing odd about a teacher carrying a roll of cardboard, Syb. And I had a scarf of yours to wrap around the bat if there was blood, but that didn't turn out to be necessary. I saved the scarf for later, and I should have left it on the Headland with the bat, but you can't think of everything, and besides, it might have looked a bit too obvious."

She looked at her hands. "I chipped my nail polish dragging Bill into position for the drill," she said. "Stupid

198

of me — I hadn't taken that into account. I knew better than to use the same polish to repair them. Had to send a kid out of the school to the local shops to get me another bottle. The little fool brought back a revolting color I wouldn't normally use, but I had no choice. Repaired my nails by painting over them. You didn't notice, did you?"

"No," Sybil said, thinking, what can I talk about? She's getting worried about the time. She said, "You've got a red leather writing case."

"Oh, you noticed that, did you? Doesn't matter, I've got rid of the paper and envelopes. Won't need to write any more letters — pity really, I enjoyed imagining Farrell's face when she read them. But I don't want to discuss that now. You're just stalling, Syb." Now she was standing, head to one side, considering the best way for Sybil to sit. "You might as well cooperate," she said with a smile. "I wouldn't want to make a mess of it for both our sakes."

"Both our sakes?" said Sybil, incredulous.

"Quick and clean, better than a slow dying. And I don't have much time, Syb, so if you'd just lean forward a bit. . . ."

Behind Lynne's smooth dark head Sybil caught a movement. She didn't dare look past her, but she knew it was Carol. Relief, love, and anger swelled in her throat. "You're pathetic!" she snapped at Lynne.

"What?"

"Well, what would you call it, Lynne? Murdering two people because you wanted to be loved. I call that pathetic."

"You're making it easy for me to kill you, Syb," said Lynne between clenched teeth.

"It's easy anyway, isn't it? You can't stand to think I've succeeded where you've failed, can you? Bill loved me,

199

Tony loved me, and Terry certainly loves me . . . but who loves you, Lynne?"

It was over in an instant. A policeman in uniform suddenly appeared from the doorway into the hall, and, as Lynne's rifle swung to cover him, Carol stepped from the back yard into the kitchen and smashed down at Lynne's hands with the butt of her gun. The rifle clattered to the floor. "Hope I haven't ruined your nail polish," said Carol.

Chapter Fourteen

Sybil's head was ringing with fatigue. She had endured the gauntlet of the media as she had entered police headquarters (statements about the death of Sir Richard's son could not be given in a suburban police station, Bourke had said to her with a satirical smile) and spent hours answering questions and making a detailed statement. Carol had been there, of course, but it was the cool, decisive, executive Carol she had first seen in the school common room the morning of Bill's murder.

Sybil wearily refused yet another cup of coffee and rested her aching head on her clasped hands. "Come on," said a silver voice, "I'll drive you home."

They avoided the reporters, leaving by a back entrance to where Carol had parked her car in the street. "Tsk," she said as they reached it, "I've got a parking ticket."

Sybil didn't respond, but slid into the seat with a silent nod of thanks. They started off, Carol driving, as usual, with smooth efficiency. The car was on the Harbour Bridge before she spoke again. "Don't laugh, but. . . ." she began, her voice uncharacteristically uncertain.

Sybil had to smile at the energy a laugh would need. "I'm too tired to laugh," she said.

"What I was going to say," said Carol casually, "was that when I knew you were in danger this morning. . . ." She shot Sybil a quick look. ". . . the things I said last night . . . they were just empty words."

Sybil was silent. Carol changed lanes abruptly and was rewarded with a blast from a horn. "Damn," she said, "you're ruining my concentration."

Sybil said, "When I realized Lynne was going to hurt me —"

"Kill you," interrupted Carol savagely. "She was going to *kill* you."

"When I realized Lynne was going to kill me, I told you I loved you, but of course, you couldn't hear."

"Couldn't I?" Carol reached over and took Sybil's hand. "Come back to my place," she said. "And before you answer, I can give you three good reasons why you should."

Sybil curled her fingers around Carol's. "Oh? They'd better be convincing."

"Okay, here they are: if you come home with me you will, first, avoid any stray reporters; second, you'll avoid Terry Clarke; third, we'll make love, and then sleep together all night and wake up to the birds and the trees and anything else you might fancy."

"Breakfast?" said Sybil, "do I get breakfast?"

Carol pursed her lips. "Only if you say you love me, and you can't live without me."

"I'll have bacon and eggs, and then toast and marmalade," said Sybil.

Publications from
BELLA BOOKS, INC.
The best in contemporary lesbian fiction

P.O. Box 10543, Tallahassee, FL 32302
Phone: 800-729-4992
www.bellabooks.com

BACK TO BASICS: A BUTCH/FEMME ANTHOLOGY
edited by Therese Szymanski—from Bella After Dark. 314 pp.
ISBN 1-931513-35-X $12.95

SURVIVAL OF LOVE by Frankie J. Jones. 236 pp. What will Jody do
when she falls in love with her best friend's daughter?
ISBN 1-931513-55-4 $12.95

DEATH BY DEATH by Claire McNab. 167 pp. 5th Denise
Cleever Thriller.   ISBN 1-931513-34-1 $12.95

CAUGHT IN THE NET by Jessica Thomas. 188 pp. A wickedly
observant story of mystery, danger, and love in Provincetown.
ISBN 1-931513-54-6 $12.95

DREAMS FOUND by Lyn Denison. 201 pp. Australian Riley embarks
on a journey to meet her birth mother . . . and gains not just a family but
the love of her life.   ISBN 1-931513-58-9 $12.95

A MOMENT'S INDISCRETION by Peggy J. Herring. 154 pp.
Jackie is torn between her better judgment and the overwhelming
attraction she feels for Valerie.   ISBN 1-931513-59-7 $12.95

IN EVERY PORT by Karin Kallmaker. 224 pp. Jessica's sexy,
adventuresome travels.   ISBN 1-931513-36-8 $12.95

TOUCHWOOD by Karin Kallmaker. 240 pp. Loving
May/December romance.   ISBN 1-931513-37-6 $12.95

WATERMARK by Karin Kallmaker. 248 pp. One burning
question . . . how to lead her back to love? ISBN 1-931513-38-4 $12.95

EMBRACE IN MOTION by Karin Kallmaker. 240 pp. A
whirlwind love affair.   ISBN 1-931513-39-2 $12.95